The Pink Palace 2:

Triple Crown Collection

The Pink Palace 2:

Triple Crown Collection

Marlon McCaulsky

www.urbanbooks.net

Urban Books, LLC
97 N18th Street
Wyandanch, NY 11798

The Pink Palace 2: Triple Crown Collection
Copyright © 2010 Triple Crown Publications, LLC

This title is published by Urban Books, LLC under a licensing agreement with Triple Crown Publications, LLC.

ISBN 13: 978-1-62286-952-7
ISBN 10: 1-62286-952-4

First Urban Books Trade Paperback Printing April 2016
First Trade Paperback Printing (October 2010)
Printed in the United States of America

10 9 8 7 6 5 4 3 2 1

Distributed by Kensington Publishing Corp.
Submit Orders to:
Customer Service
400 Hahn Road
Westminster, MD 21157-4627
Phone: 1-800-733-3000
Fax: 1-800-659-2436

Prologue

Back Again for the First Time

Atlanta, GA
NICOLE "NIKKI" BELL

It had been three years since I'd been back here at
The Pink Palace. It felt like a lifetime ago. I was a different person now than I was back then. Back then you
couldn't tell me nothing. I was hustling these tricks,
shaking my ass, and selling my body to the man with
the most cash. I was doing anything and everything
for the dollar. God, I was so stupid back then.

It wasn't until I got caught up in my own hustle and
got my ass kicked by a nigga who didn't give a shit
about me, and I almost died as a result of my stupid
state of mind, that I realized how foolish I was being
and changed my life.

So you ask, why was I back there? Because less than
a month ago, my whole world was ripped apart, and
now I had to do what I had to do in order to protect the
man I loved.

After I quit stripping three years ago, I started to live
my life with the man I loved with all my heart, Andre
Wade. Dre had quit the game, too, and started his
own business in midtown called A-Town Grillz. And
more importantly, we had a baby boy. Tyler changed
everything for us. I became a mother, and Dre was

going to be the father to Tyler that he never had. We were starting to live our lives together, and we bought a house in College Park in the Stone Ridge subdivision. We decided to take our time and plan the wedding that I never thought I would have.

My cousin Janelle, who I loved dearly, was going to be my maid of honor. She was going to be mines like I was hers when she got married to Jayson.

I was so proud of her. Janelle had always been the strongest of us. I never told her this, but she had always inspired me to do better. I wondered what she'd think if she saw me now.

But at any rate, life was going perfect—or that's what I thought until Dre started to receive mysterious phone calls. Dre always seemed to be upset after he got off the phone. I finally decided to ask him about it.

"Dre, baby, what's going on?" I asked him.

He smiled. "It's nothing, baby."

"It didn't sound like nothing. Who's been calling you?"

"Nobody important. Just some niggas I used to run with back in the day," Dre coolly replied as he picked up Tyler off the couch where he fell asleep.

"What do they want?"

"Like I said, nothing important," Dre said to me as he took Tyler to his room and laid him down in his crib. "The only thing I'm looking forward to is getting your pretty behind down to Miami this weekend."

Whatever it was, Dre didn't want to talk about it, and I didn't want to push it and start a fight right before we went on a mini vacation to South Beach. Besides, if Dre didn't want to talk about something, he wasn't gonna talk about it.

"Okay, well, Penny said she'd watch Tyler for us. I don't know how she's gonna deal with both Tyler and her bad-ass little Tarius, but she said it's no problem," I told him.

"Good. Our flight leaves at twelve thirty tomorrow, so we'll drop him off at nine." Dre saw a concerned expression on my face. "Nikki, you don't got anything to worry about, okay?"

"Okay, baby, but you know you can tell me anything. I love you."

"I know, Nikki. I love you too." Dre kissed my lips.

I knew Dre had not gone back to hustling, but he still knew people in the game. Dre had even told me that the money we made from A-Town Grillz was more than enough and he didn't need to hustle anymore. Between selling custom grills and jewelry, CDs, and a small fashion boutique I ran in the store, we were able to buy our house in College Park.

But in my heart, I knew there was something else going on that Dre wasn't telling me. I decided not to press the issue. I would just concentrate on enjoying myself in Miami with my man.

We packed our suitcases that night, and the next day, we dropped Tyler over at Penny's house over in Morrow. She still stayed in the same house Janelle and I used to stay in with her. Penny had quit dancing at The Pink Palace a year ago and I hired her at our store. After we dropped off Tyler, we drove to Hartsfield Atlanta Airport, and we were off to Miami.

After I had Tyler, Dre made it a point to take little mini vacations together so we wouldn't get caught up in just living life but also enjoying it. We had the money, so why not?

We got to Miami two and half hours later, and Dre rented us a 2011 Lexus Coupe and we drove down Ocean Drive to The Regent hotel on Miami Beach. This was a lavish suite with a beautiful view of the beach from the balcony. Dre was doing it big for me, and that's why I loved him so much.

"This is what I needed," I said to Dre as I stood on the balcony and stared at the blue water.

Dre walked up behind me and put his arms around me. "And you're all I need right here," Dre said as his big hands rubbed my breasts.

I leaned my head back and kissed him. "You're all I ever needed, too, baby."

"You wanna go down there?"

"Yeah, I want to show you my new bikini I got from the Mychael Knight collection."

"I can't wait to see you in it," Dre replied eagerly.

Dre went back inside and changed into a pair of black shorts and flip-flops and went down to the lobby to wait for me. I got changed into my exclusive Mychael Knight blue two-piece bikini.

I was shocked at how well my body got back into shape after I had Tyler. It was like I never had a baby. In fact, my breasts went up a couple sizes after I had him, and it helped me fill out this bikini.

After I got dressed, I took the elevator down to the lobby. When the door opened, I stepped off, and Dre's eyes lit up.

"Sweet Jesus! Nikki, you look . . . wow," Dre droned.

"Just the reaction I was hoping for."

"Girl, I'm scared to take you out there."

"No need to be. I'm all yours."

We headed out to the beach, and just like Dre feared, all eyes were on me. Guys watched me walk on the beach, and my bikini showed all my sexy curves from my incredible eye-popping cleavage, long brown legs, and my round ass that bounced to its own beat.

But I wasn't the only one getting stares and looks. Women were ogling Dre like the beefcake he was. Dre's sexy muscular chest and six-pack were hard enough to lick whip cream off.

I had to admit the women here on South Beach were gorgeous too. I even caught Dre sneaking a peek at a couple of Jamaican chicks. I couldn't even get mad at him, because they were stunning. It was a good thing we didn't live there, or I'd have to fight a chick every day!

Later that night, Dre took me to a nightclub called Club B.E.D. If a man couldn't get a woman in bed there, then he should just stop trying altogether. The atmosphere in the club was young and sexy, and I was the sexist woman in the spot. I wore a red spaghetti strap dress, matching Prada shoes, and my MAC makeup was flawless. Dre was pimped out in black Avirex Jeans and an Avirex logo printed polo. He was laced with his long, platinum chain, iced-out Rolex, and his Atlanta fitted on his head.

Dre ordered us some Patrón. The club was filled with ballers making it rain on pretty women and hustlers flossin' their ice. The DJ dropped Usher's "Love in this Club," and that's what it looked like everybody was doing on the dance floor as the women grinded on the men. So you know I had no choice but to put it on Dre in my own special way.

The club had plush, soft beds, and I made Dre lay back as I straddled him and rode him like a jockey. I grinded my hips back and forth in a sexy dance, giving him a preview of what he was going to get later that night.

"Oh, shit, Nikki," Dre exclaimed as I felt his dick become rock hard underneath me. "You gonna make me tear your ass up right here in this club!"

"Well, we are on a bed, and it wouldn't be the first time we've made love in a club," I purred to him.

Dre grinned. "Hmmm, yeah, that was the shit."

"That was nothing compared to what I got in mind for you tonight," I said and gave him a kiss as my tongue played with his.

Once again, I gained the attention of some men watching as my dress rose up and exposed my red thong. We decided to get up and dance. The DJ put on Mario's "Music For Love," and I let the baseline hit me. I was putting it on Dre like I was his personal stripper. Well, actually I was. I bent over and gyrated my ass on his crotch, and once again, all eyes were on me as niggas were taking notes.

After a few more songs and a few more shots of Patrón, we went and sat back down on the bed.

"Baby, I gotta go to the ladies room."

"A'ight, baby. Hurry back."

"You know I will," I replied as I walked to the restroom. I had to pee really badly. I guess that Patrón just ran through me. Must have been the reason I was feeling so horny!

After I came out of the ladies room, I saw a dude that was watching me on the dance floor. I knew what he had in mind, and I tried to avoid him, but homie was on a mission.

"Hey, momma, where you going?" he said to me. "I got what you need right here, baby girl." He smiled and showed me his fucked-up yellow teeth. This mutha-fucka looked like Eddie Griffin on crack!

"Back to my man," I confirmed to him, walking away. This nigga had the nerve to grab my arm! Looked like I was gonna have to bust a nigga head.

"Why you running away? I seen the way you were grinding on that nigga, and I just wanna holla."

I snatched my arm away from him. "Don't you ever put ya hands on me! What the fuck is wrong with you?" I yelled at him.

He grinned. "No disrespect. I just think you can do better."

"Negro, please. You better be glad my man ain't see you touch me or you'd be fucked up right now!" I turned to walk away.

"Drunk-ass stripper bitch!"

Now why did he have to say that shit to me of all people? I turned back around and glared at him. "You know what your problem is? You a weak-ass nigga. Learn how to talk to a woman. Weak-ass rap. And fix ya mutherfucking grill before you try to talk to a chick with them yellow, rotten teeth," I yelled and walked away.

Dre was getting his drink on when I got back to him.

"Hey, baby, I'm ready to go."

"Already? You sure? We just got here," Dre asked me, confused.

"Yeah, I'm sure."

"Something wrong?

"No, I just wanna go back to the hotel now."

"A'ight, lets go," Dre replied and got up off the bed.

We left the club. I didn't tell Dre about what happened in the club, because I didn't want Dre to kill that fool. Plus, I was already pissed off. I was having a good time with my man, and that bitch-ass nigga had to bring me down.

We drove back to the hotel, and I went out on the balcony to get some fresh air and stare at the ocean. The view was beautiful at night. I shouldn't have let that nigga get to me when I was there in that beautiful city with my man.

"Hey, baby? You okay," Dre asked.

I turned and looked at him. "Yeah, I'm sorry I was short with you at the club."

"Don't worry about it. I need to talk to you alone anyway."

"What about?"

"Have a seat," Dre said as he gestured to the chair on the balcony.

I sat in the chair as Dre stood in front of me. "Nikki, for the past three years we've been kickin' it, and I've never felt this happy. We've been through hell and back and we're still here. You gave me a son, a little me. You're my lady. You've always been the one," Dre said to me sincerely.

"What are you saying, Dre?"

"I know we've talked about getting married after we had Tyler. In my mind, you're already my wife, but I just wanna make it official," Dre affirmed as he got down on one knee in front of me and took out a little black box.

I couldn't believe this was finally happening.

"You mean everything to me, and I wanna give you the world. Nicole Bell, will you marry me?" Dre asked as he opened the box and I saw the biggest diamond on a platinum ring I'd ever seen. I was speechless and just stared at the ring. "Nikki? This is the part where you're suppose to say something."

"What? Oh, yes! Oh God, yes!" I shouted, excited as Dre smiled from ear to ear.

He slid the ring on my finger and my eyes began to water up. I kissed Dre's lips. This was the most perfect moment of my life. I never thought I would ever be engaged to a man. After stripping for six years, I just thought that marriage wasn't meant for a woman like me.

As we kissed, all those hurt feelings I felt went away, and the horny mistress in me came back out. Dre's tongue danced with mine, and I felt my pussy get wet. He kissed my neck and shoulders as he slid my spaghetti strap off my shoulder and exposed my titty. My nipples were stiff as Dre sucked on them.

"Lets go back inside, baby," Dre suggested to me, and I had a better idea.

"No, let's do it right here," I hummed with a naughty grin on my face.

"What? You serious?"

"Uh-huh," I replied as I opened my legs for him.

Dre slid his hands up my inner thighs and massaged them. My pussy was pulsating with excitement as I felt myself become wetter. Dre pulled my thong to the side and rubbed his thumb up and down my clit, using my wetness to lube me up. Then he took his thumb and licked it clean.

"Just as sweet as ever," Dre said and went back and pulled my thong down.

The cool sea breeze on this hot summer night made me feel even hornier as Dre licked my walls. I bit my bottom lip as I felt his saliva mix with my wetness. Dre pulled my ass to the edge as I leaned back in the chair. His tongue flicked my clit back and forth, bringing my orgasm closer to the edge. I rotated my hips up and down as my pussy throbbed. That was when Dre unleashed his "Tasmanian Devil Tongue" on my pussy.

"Oh, fuck! Aaaahhhh," I shouted at the top of my lungs, not caring who heard me.

Dre's tongue swirled around my clit as he slurped my juices up. My legs trembled uncontrollably as I climaxed.

"Ah, ah, Dre! Please . . ."

Dre pulled back, wearing my juices on his face, and smiled. I stared in his eyes and smiled back as my orgasm rushed over me. No words were needed as I tried to catch my breath.

Dre took off his Avirex polo, reveling his muscular, sculpted chest. He stood up, unbuckled his belt, and pulled down his pants and underwear. That elephant trunk dick of his stood out like a pole. Damn, just looking at his body made me wet all over again. My pussy was still throbbing from his tongue-lashing.

"Stand up and turn around and face the ocean," Dre commanded, and I obeyed.

I put my hands on the balcony handrail and bent over, pushing my ass out. Dre stood behind me and smacked his hard dick against my ass.

"Ow! You so hard," I turned and said to him.

"And your ass is so soft." Dre took the head of his dick and rubbed it up and down my pussy. Then he slowly pushed his shaft in me, inch by inch.

"Aahh," I moaned as he slowly stroked me from the back.

Dre knew how to work me slow and deep, making me feel every inch of his stiffness. I threw it back on him, tightening my pussy, gripping his dick when he pushed into me. There I was, on the sixth floor of a hotel balcony, with my dress around my waist and my right titty hanging out, getting hit doggie style by my fiancé. My pussy was jumping, feeling his manhood rise inside me. I felt my pussy cum on his dick.

"Dammit, Dre. I love the way you fuck me," I said, out of breath.

Dre proceeded to hit me harder and faster, gripping onto my hips. My pussy began to make that squishing sound as I began to moan at the top of my lungs. My hands held on tightly to the railing as Dre pounded away.

"Ah! Ah! Oh God!"

I look out at the beach and see passersby looking up at our balcony performance. They were too far away and it was too dark for them to really see us anyway. Besides, I didn't mind being a ho for Dre, because soon I would be his wife.

Dre withdrew out of me, and my legs wobbled as I held on to the railing for balance.

"Let's go to the bed, baby," Dre said to me as he stood behind me. His dick was dripping with my cum, glistening in the moonlight.

"That sounds good, but I can't walk, baby."

"You won't have to," Dre said as he walked over to me and picked me up.

I wrapped my legs around his waist. Dre put his hand under my ass then took his hard dick and plunged it back in me. Dre pumped me deeply, kissing my lips as he walked us back into our room and laid me on the bed, careful not to take himself out of me. Then I let my legs spread farther as Dre lay on top of me and made love to me.

Dre made love to me for hours before emptying himself inside me. My orgasm lasted another ten minutes, until my pussy finally calmed down.

After Dre was done having his way with me, I curled up on my side and went to sleep. I was so drained. Literality. Dre spooned up behind me, and the bed was so soft. Damn, there was nothing like a real man to make a woman feel so good.

After a while, I didn't feel Dre behind me, and then I heard him on the phone on the balcony. His voice was raised, arguing with someone. I listened to him speak.

"I don't give a damn what you think, nigga! I paid you back every dime I owed you," Dre yelled into his phone. "No! What you need to do is stop calling my motherfucking phone, nigga! I don't owe you shit anymore. . . . Whatever, nigga! It's like that? Well, suck my dick," Dre yelled and hung up his phone.

Dre was irate, and I knew in my heart that this was going to be a major problem for both of us. I sat up in bed and waited for Dre to come in.

He walked back in the room and saw me, and we shared an awkward silence.

Dre sighed. "You heard everything?"

"Yeah. What's going on, Dre?"

"I didn't want you to worry about this shit," Dre said regrettably.

"Dre, if I'm going to be your wife, then you have to be honest with me or this will never work. Are you hustling again?"

"No. I haven't been selling for over three years now."

"Then what's going on? Who do you owe money to?"

"I don't owe money to nobody. Not anymore," Dre clarified. "Back when I got arrested, the police seized all of my supply, and I owed my supplier a lot of money."

"How much money?" I inquired.

"A little over two hundred thousand, but for the last two years, I've been paying him back every week from the profit we've made from the store."

I frowned. "Why didn't you tell me this before?"

"Because it was my problem, and you were having a baby, and it was something I had under control."

"And now? What's changed?"

"This nigga Malachi Turner says that I owe him interest, and he wants me to pay him another hundred thousand. What kind of bullshit interest rate is that?"

"Who's Malachi Turner?"

"This nigga that was supplying me from Decatur. He has a connection to a drug lord down in Colombia. This nigga is starting to take over most of Atlanta, becoming the number one dope supplier. But this nigga is trying to extort me, and I ain't gonna let nobody do that to me," Dre explained and sat next to me in bed.

"So what are we gonna do?"

"I've been talking to my nigga Polo, and he said he would see what he can do to get Malachi off my back."

"And if he can't?" I asked him and Dre stared at me.

"Then I'ma have to do what I gotta do."

"What about Tyler, Dre? What about me? We need you, baby. I thought we left all this bullshit behind us. I can't lose you now."

"Nikki, you ain't gonna lose me, 'cause I ain't going nowhere. You're going to be my wife, and I'm going to make sure we straight for life," Dre affirmed and caressed my face. "Come on. Let's go back to bed."

Dre got back into bed with me and held me close, but I just knew that this shit with Malachi wasn't going to be as easy to handle as Dre said it would be. Why was this happening now? I just wanted to be happy with Dre and Tyler, so why couldn't I have that?

It had been two weeks since we left Miami, and life had gone back to normal. I started to make plans for our wedding, and we set a date for four months later. I decided to hire a wedding planer instead of driving myself mad trying to arrange everything.

I was at the shop working with Penny, and Janelle came by to visit me. Like I said before, I was so proud of my little cousin Janelle. She graduated from Georgia State University, got married to Jayson, and was now a Production Assistant working at Radio One, Hot 107.9. She didn't let her past as a stripper define her life. She was still so beautiful, even dressed causally in a pair of Dereon jeans and a pink Dereon hoodie and Air Force Ones.

"Girl, I'm so excited about your wedding. When are you gonna pick out your dress?" Janelle demanded to know.

"Dress? I'm still trying to figure out what type of food I want at the reception!"

"Why are you worried? What's the point of hiring a wedding planner if you're gonna be stressed?" Janelle asked me.

"I don't know. I guess I'm just nervous."

"You don't got anything to be nervous about. You and Dre are going to be happy together for years," Penny said to me.

"I know. It just seems too good to be true."

"Is there something wrong, Nikki?" Janelle queried, sensing there was something else on my mind.

"No, I'm fine. I just want everything to be perfect like you are with Jayson."

"Jayson and me are far from perfect, but he's a wonderful man. We make it work. And now he's ready for us to start having kids."

"Are you ready?" Penny asked her. "'Cause I just got one, and Tarius is a handful."

"Tarius done been here before with his little bad ass self! He's gonna be getting Tyler in all sorts of trouble when they get older. But, J, are you ready for kids?" I asked her.

"I am. It's just I have a good chance of moving up quickly at my job, and I don't know if I can have a baby now and still move ahead," Janelle said to us.

"Janelle, I know you can do anything you put your mind to. Don't let a job stop you and Jayson from starting a family if that's what you want."

"Thank you, Nikki," Janelle replied and hugged me.

We continued to talk about our lives and my wedding plans for the next few minutes.

Dre came in the store, holding Tyler. Tyler was two and a half years old, and was a daddy's boy already. He loved Dre so much; sometimes he'd cry until his daddy came and picked him up.

"Hey, y'all," Dre said to us.

"What's up, Dre?" Janelle replied and went over and picked up Tyler. She loved him as if he was her son too.

"Hey, big man! How you doing?" Janelle talked to Tyler and kissed his chubby cheeks. Tyler loved to be kissed, especially from Janelle. He was going to be a little playa when he grew up.

"What y'all up to?" Dre asked and gave me a kiss.

"Nothing. Just having girl talk."

He smirked. "Y'all talking about sex, huh? That's all y'all women do."

"No, that's not all we do. You just nasty," Penny said to him.

"I know you know I'm nasty. I bet Nikki be giving y'all details blow by blow," Dre said braggingly.

"Shut up, boy! I don't be talking about your narrow ass," I lied. We did talk about sex, but that was done when we all had a drink or two at lunch! "We were talking about our wedding."

"Yeah, Dre, you better enjoy your last few months of freedom. Anyway, I gotta get going. I'll call y'all later." Janelle kissed Tyler and gave him to me.

"All right, girl. Later." Janelle walked out of the store.

"You ready to go too, Nikki?" Dre asked me.

"Yeah, Penny, you'll be all right here by yourself?"

"Girl, I'll be fine," Penny confirmed to me.

Dre, Tyler, and I went outside to Dre's black Cutlas Deville. I swear he loved that car almost as much as me.

A-Town Grillz was on the corner of Spring Street and Mitchell, the small business part of Midtown Atlanta. I put Tyler in his car seat in the back and got in on the passenger side.

"Damn, Dre, I forgot Tyler's baby bag behind the counter inside."

"Don't worry. I'll get it," Dre said and got out and went back inside the store.

Dre came back out of the store with the bag, and that was when everything started to move in slow motion for me. A white Crown Victoria car screeched out in front of Dre, and he dropped the baby bag and started to run the other way. Then I hear gunshots ring out.

"Dre!" I cried as he collapsed on the sidewalk.

The white car sped off down Spring Street. I got up out of the car and ran toward Dre. He was lying on his stomach, and I saw a gunshot wound in his back.

At that point, I think I was freaking out. I got down on the ground and held Dre in my arms.

"Help me! Please, somebody help me!" I screamed at the top of my lungs.

Penny came out of the store and ran over to me. "Oh God! Nikki!" Penny yelled, crying.

"Call the paramedics!"

Penny dialed on her cell phone. A few people on the streets stopped and stared at me on the ground with Dre.

"Dre, Dre . . . baby, please wake up," I pleaded with him, but his eyes wouldn't open. "Please don't leave me. Please." I could feel the blood coming from Dre's body on me. Then I heard Tyler crying from inside the car. Penny ran over to the car to comfort him.

My worst fear had come to life. The next few minutes were a blur, as both cops and paramedics crowded the area.

The paramedics took Dre to Grady Memorial Hospital.

Janelle drove me to the hospital. Tears just rolled from my eyes as I sat in the waiting room and asked

God why. I was planning to have the wedding of my dreams, and now I might have to plan a funeral for the man I loved more than anything else in the world.

The police, of course, asked me what I saw, and I told them what happened. I couldn't identify the two guys I saw in the car. The only thing I knew was that Dre had beef with this Malachi Turner, but I didn't tell the police that.

"Nikki, I'm so sorry," Janelle said to me.

"What am I going to do now?" I asked feebly.

"It's going to be okay, Nikki. Dre's a strong man. He'll pull through this."

"We both are gonna be here for you and Tyler," Penny added.

I knew that they would be by my side, but that still didn't change the fact that Dre was shot right in front of me and they weren't gonna stop until he was dead. Dre was in a coma. The doctors said he could wake up the next day or next year. It all depended on how fast his body could heal itself.

I sat in his room, holding his hand as tears rolled down my face. They were not tears of sadness, because I had already exhausted them, but my tears were of anger. I was furious that Dre was shot down in the streets and the police weren't doing anything to find who did it. Dre being an ex dope boy was reason enough for them to drag their feet on this case.

Dre's friend Polo came to the hospital to see him, and I was sure he had to know who was behind Dre's attempted murder.

"Hey, Polo," I greeted him as we stood by Dre's bed.

"Hey, Nikki. I know this is a hard time for you. I'm sorry this happened," Polo said to me.

"I know. But you do know who did this, don't you?"

Polo shook his head. "Nikki . . ."

"You do! Dre said some guy name Malachi Turner was trying to extort him."

"Nikki, you don't need to be talking about this now."

"Then when?" I snapped in a raised tone. "He did this to Dre and you know it."

Polo looked at me sadly. He was one of Dre's best friends. "Yeah, Malachi did it."

"Then what are you gonna do about it?"

He crinkled his eyebrows. "What you want me to do?"

"Kill him. That's what I want you to do," I coldly retorted.

Polo shook his head in disbelief. "Nikki, you don't know who Malachi is or just how powerful he is."

"I don't give a fuck who he is! All I know is you're Dre's best friend and you're too much of a coward to kill the nigga that did this to him," I spit angrily. Polo frowned because I was calling him out, but I didn't give a fuck at this point.

"Nikki, Malachi is the biggest dope man in Atlanta. He ain't some corner boy. This nigga got an army around him. Ain't nobody that stupid enough to try him."

I stared at him suspiciously. "He's supplying you too?"

"Yeah, he does. Listen, Nikki, this nigga is huge. He even owns The Pink Palace. Nigga is paid," Polo explained to me.

"He owns The Pink Palace?" I said, shocked.

"You didn't know? I guess Dre ain't wanna tell you. Yeah, he runs the place himself. I can't help you on this one, Nikki. I'm sorry." Polo looked at Dre's unconscious body in the bed then walked away.

It became clear to me that nobody was going to try Malachi—not the police, and definitely not Polo. But I couldn't just let go.

For the next two weeks, I was at the hospital by Dre's side with Tyler. Penny was running the store for me. I tried to move on, but I couldn't. All I could think about was what Malachi did to him. Sometimes I would just stare at Tyler and see Dre in him and cry. I just felt like there was this hole in my chest, and the only thing I could fill it with was rage.

Why was this all happening to me? Why did this happen to us? We were going to be a real family. Dre was going to be my husband.

1

The Baddest Bitch

Atlanta, GA
JACQUELINE "JASMINE" DAWSON

The spotlight shone on the long black runway stage. The smell of liquor and smoke lingered in the air throughout the dimly lit club. My skin tingled with excitement as my body glowed from the baby oil I rubbed all over me. My breasts stood firm in my skimpy bikini top, imprinting my erect nipples underneath.

I stepped out on stage in my five hundred–dollar red Prada shoes like a supermodel and gave the crowd of men ogling my curvy body my signature walk on the runway. It was more of a strut than a walk. Nobody could match my swagger as I grabbed the chrome pole and pulled my body upside down like a trained athlete. I wrapped my long, smooth, golden brown legs around the pole and swung around until I touched the ground.

The crowd of horny men loved the way I flexed my body to the beat of Ray J's "Sexy Can I." I dropped into a split and made my ass clap, and twenties and fifties flew like confetti on the stage.

I stared in the eyes of this one dude and licked my full, succulent lips. He was hypnotized. Without a word, I mentally commanded him to empty his wallet for me. Plus the fact that I took off my bikini top made him my slave. It was amazing how stupid men got when they saw titties.

This one guy decided to "make it rain" and showered me with ones, tens, and a couple of twenties. I guess he thought all women were impressed by that, but it was the dumbest thing I'd ever seen! You think a woman would throw money on the ground for a nigga? Dumb-ass!

I'd been dancing at The Pink Palace for only ten months, and I was already the top-dollar bitch in the club! I had just made over a grand in less time than it took to fill out a job application.

I walked out front and saw this new girl that called herself Kandi. She did look sweet enough to lick all right. She was a young, tight thing, just like I liked them!

Oh, no. I saw her doing a table dance for the nasty little pervert Reggie. He was Malachi's little brother and he walked around there like he owned the place. Half the time he was up in VIP trying to fuck with the girls or walking through the locker room like he was an inspector trying to look at everybody's ass for free. Nasty little troll was always scratching his crotch. That was why nobody with common sense and 20/20 vision would fuck with his ugly self. He might have been Malachi's brother, but he ain't had the money, power, or respect his brother did.

Poor Kandi didn't know any better. He was slapping her ass so hard I could hear it from across the room. She was just smiling like she enjoyed it, but that shit had to sting. Great. Now he just pulled her down in his lap and was rubbing all up on her. She was trying to stop him from digging his fingers under her bikini thong. The bouncer wasn't gonna say nothing to Malachi's little brother, so I decided I better check this stupid nigga.

"Come on, stop," Kandi said to him, but he didn't.

"Damn you got a fatty, girl. Let me get a sniff," Reggie said to her.

"Reggie! You didn't hear what she just said?"

He stopped and smiled at me.

"Hey, Jasmine, why don't you join us and let's get this shit really crunk!"

"How about I tell Malachi you're fucking with the girls again?" I shot back at him and he glared at me.

"Get the fuck up," he spits to Kandi, and she did quickly and started to walk away.

"Hold up. Don't leave so fast," I said to her, and she looked at me, confused and scared. "This nigga owes you for your lap dance."

"What? Bitch, please." Reggie rolled his eyes.

"Pay her . . . now," I said to him seriously.

Reggie glared at me as he pulled out a wad of cash, peeled off a ten, and gave it to her.

"Lap dances cost more than that," I informed him. He cut his eyes at me and then gave Kandi a twenty.

"Here. Now piss off!"

"Fuck you too," I snapped at him and took Kandi backstage with me.

"Thank you for helping me," Kandi said and smiled.

"No problem, sweetie. Don't ever let me see you fucking with that dusty nigga again. Just because his brother owns The Palace don't make him shit," I explained to her.

"Okay," she said shyly. She had to be barely eighteen, if that. She looked kinda like Keisha Knight Pulliam, only a little sexier in a blue two-piece and stilettos.

"You heading out?"

"Yeah, my feet are killing me. Thank you, Jasmine."

"Don't worry about it. Just remember what I told you." I gave her a hug and seductively brushed a few stray hairs from her face.

She smiled and then turned and walked toward the locker room backstage, but then she turned and looked back at me. Gotcha! Pretty young thing didn't know it yet, but she was gonna be mines soon.

I looked around the club and noticed that there was nothing left there but some small-time niggas. I'd already made my paper for the night, so I decided to bounce out of there too. Then I saw the man himself come through the club doors. Unlike his ugly-ass brother Reggie, Malachi just looked like money. Don't get me wrong; Malachi was ugly too, but his money just made him a lot sexier.

Malachi was a big man, built like a linebacker. His shoulders were wide, and his chest was solid, so you know his $3,000 black Italian suit was tailor-made to fit his hulking frame. His hair was cut in a low Caesar fade with endless waves. His skin was a smooth, jet-black complexion, and his eyes were an intense dark brown. He intimidated even the hardest nigga that thought he was a thug.

Fear was in some ways better than respect, although I didn't feel either when I was around him. The power of my pussy made him a different man behind closed doors.

He strolled in with his niggas around him. Big Bump was his bodyguard, and Ricky was one of his boys that ran the corners for him. His eyes scanned the room, and he saw me and gave me that lustful glare. He then made his way up the stairs to his office. It looked like I was gonna get some overtime that night.

MALACHI TURNER

All eyes were on me as I walked into the club. Some looked at me with respect, but most of them with fear. That was better. That made niggas easier to control. This was my club, my world, so that made me a god.

As I glanced across the club, I saw that everything was running smooth, like a well-oiled stripper on a pole. The DJ was spinning a new track from Ludacris, and there were two girls on stage, shaking they asses like they was supposed to. But then I saw my number one rump-shaker standing at the bar, looking finer than a bitch. Jasmine. Since she'd been dancing there, business had been at an all-time high. Just seeing her in that bikini made a nigga's dick rock hard.

But I had other things on my mind than pussy. I spotted my idiot little brother, Reggie, fucking with some girls at a table. Stupid nigga tought with his dick more than the got-damn sense he was born with. He better had taken care of that shit I told him to do.

He saw me and straightened himself up. I headed upstairs to my office with Ricky behind me. Bump stood outside my door. Ricky had a seat in front of my mahogany desk, and I walked to the glass window behind my chair and looked down at the club. I saw Reggie coming upstairs to see me.

"Do you think Reggie got that shit taken care of?" Ricky asked me.

"He better have. Did you get that shit from Jorge?"

"Yeah, right on time as usual. Detective Raymond made sure we stayed off the radar."

Big Bump opened my door and let Reggie in.

"What's up, bruh?" He then turned and saw Ricky and scowled. He made no secret of his dislike of him.

Reggie thought that just because he was my brother that he should be running the corners instead of Ricky. He was my brother, but he was also a fuck-up. Ricky handled whatever I told him to do without screw-ups.

"You can't say hello, Reggie?" Ricky said to him sarcastically.

"Rick," Reggie said dryly.

"Did you get that thing done, Reggie?" I said to him.

"Hell yeah. That nigga Dre ain't gonna be a problem for ya anymore."

"Good."

"I told ya I would handle that bitch. You should let me handle more shit for you, bruh," Reggie bragged and looked at Ricky.

Ricky smiled and shook his head. "You got something to say to me, Reggie?"

"If I got something to say to *you*, nigga, then I say it," Ricky informed him with a lot more bass in his voice.

"Look at this nigga. Just because you took care of some small-time nigga for Malachi, you think you can do what I do? You silly, nigga." Ricky laughed at him.

"Fuck you, Rick! Dre was one of the biggest dealers in Atlanta, and I handled that nigga! Keep on talking shit and I'll handle yo' bitch ass too!"

Ricky stood up and got in Reggie's face. If Reggie wasn't my brother, Ricky would've put a bullet in his head by now. Ricky had killed niggas for much less in the streets.

"You can't handle shit, nigga. That's why Malachi keeps your bitch ass up in this club where he can watch yo' baby ass."

Ricky was correct in his assessment. Reggie was too immature to be left on his own in the streets. I promised our mother I would take care of his ass before she passed away, but with Reggie taking care of Dre for me, he was starting to prove himself for me.

"Both of you niggas shut the fuck up." I took a seat behind my desk and pulled out an already rolled blunt from my desk. "You did good, Reggie. You just do as I tell you and I'll give you more shit to do in the future."

My private line started to ring, and I looked at the caller ID. "Both of y'all get the fuck out. I gotta take this call."

They both walked out of my office, and I picked up the phone.

"Hello."

"Hey, daddy," my six-year-old daughter, Courtney, said.

"What are you doing up so late?"

"I couldn't sleep, Daddy. Mommy said it would be all right if I called you. When are you coming by?"

That bitch of a mother of hers knew I wouldn't be back over in Dunwoody until that weekend. She did this shit on purpose to mess with me. She knew Courtney was the only way she could see me on a regular basis.

"Baby girl, Daddy has a lot of work to do, so I won't make it over there until later."

"Okay," she said sadly.

"But don't worry, sweetheart. When I see you, I'm gonna have a surprise for you."

"Really?" she asked, excited.

"Yes, really. Now go to bed and I'll call you in the morning."

"Okay, Daddy."

"I love you, Courtney."

"I love you too, Daddy."

"Okay, now put your mother on the phone." I looked down out the window and saw Jasmine sitting at the bar, looking up at my window. I gestured for her to come up. I heard Courtney giving the phone to her mother, Latoya.

"Yeah," she said dryly.

"What did I tell you about putting shit in Courtney's head?" I growled at her.

"I just told her if she wants to see her daddy then call him," Latoya snapped with attitude.

"You gonna stop playing games with me, Latoya! You gonna stop that shit or—"

"Or what, nigga? I'm the mother of yo' child! You should be here with us instead of that damn club fucking wit' them strippers!"

"Don't forget that I met your ass in a strip club, shaking yo' ass too, bitch! And if you wanna keep living in that big-ass house that I'm paying for, you do what the fuck I tell you to," I reminded her.

There was silence on the line as she thought about what I'd just told her.

Big Bump opened my door and let Jasmine in.

"I just want us to be a family again, Malachi. You know I love you," Latoya said to me.

Jasmine walked over and sat her sexy, fat round ass on my desk.

"You just remember what I said and there won't be any problems," I said and hung up.

Jasmine spun her fat ass around on my desk and faced me. "Wifey stressing you out?" she said, teasing me.

"She not my bumbaclot wife."

"I hate seeing you so upset, Malachi," she said and kicked off her red Prada shoes. Then she seductively rubbed her feet up my slacks and found my rock hard dick. Damn, she was so fucking sexy.

I grabbed her long, thick leg. Her calves were muscular, sculpted from hours of dancing.

"What you got for me, baby?" she asked.

I pulled six Ben Franklins out my pocket and dropped it on my desk. She skillfully scooped it up and tucked it under her bikini top. Then she dropped between my legs and unzipped my slacks and pulled out my dick.

She darted her tongue around the tip then licked my sensitive spot just below the head. She sent shivers up and down my shaft. Her technique was the shit!

I leaned back in my chair, and she deep-throated me and milked my dick for the next hour. She served me like everybody else. Like I said, this was my world, and I was a god.

2

Paranoia

Atlanta, GA

NIKKI

As much as I hated to leave Dre's side, I had to get back to Penny at the shop. Between Penny and Janelle coming in helping her out, business was still coming into the store, but bills needed to be paid.

It had been one month since Dre went into a coma, and the hospital was sending me bills left and right. We didn't have heath insurance. I was lucky Dre and I had some paper saved away for Tyler's college fund. I hated to touch it, but I didn't have much choice.

What the hell am I gonna do now? I thought as I rode down the elevator in Emory Hospital. *How can I run the business, take care of Tyler, and continue to pay Dre's medical expenses before we're completely broke? I hope Obama can get this universal health care plan past them fools in Washington.*

I walked through the walkway from the lobby to the parking garage and took another elevator to the fourth level. As I was walking to Dre's black Cutlass Deville, I heard somebody bumping T.I.'s *Paper Trail* album. I looked down the garage and saw a black Escalade on 24-inch rims. The windows were a dark tint, so I couldn't see who was inside. I got a bad vibe for some reason, and I got in the Cutlass and started it up.

I pulled out of the parking space and drove by the Escalade. Nothing happened. Maybe I was still just a little paranoid.

I got to the shop and saw Penny and Janelle holding down the fort for me. They didn't know how much I loved them for stepping in and helping me like that. Penny was checking a lady out at the counter, and Janelle walked over to me and gave me a hug.

"What's up, cuz?" Janelle said to me.

"Same old shit."

"Dre's still the same condition?"

"Yeah. The doctors are still telling me there's no telling when Dre could come out of this."

"I'm so sorry, Nikki," Janelle said to me sincerely.

"You don't need to be. That muthafucka Malachi is the one that's gonna be sorry."

"Malachi? Who's that?" Janelle asked me.

I shouldn't have let his name come out of my mouth.

"Is he the one that did this to Dre?"

"Yes."

"Why didn't you tell the police?"

"I don't have any proof he did it. Plus I don't trust them fuckin' cops either." Shit. I shouldn't have said that knowing that her husband Jayson was a cop too. "I'm sorry, Janelle. I know Jayson is a good man."

"It's okay, Nikki. Who is this Malachi?"

"He's the new owner of The Pink Palace," I said to her, and Janelle shook her head. It seemed like a lifetime ago we both used to dance up in there. Janelle had done her best to put that place behind her, and here I was bringing it back up. "He and Dre did some business together back when Dre was hustling. When Dre got busted, he still owed him some money. For the last three years, Dre has been paying him back, and after he paid him what he owed, Malachi wanted to extort more money from him."

"Let me guess: Dre refused to give him any more money and Malachi went after him," Janelle said.

"Yeah. Piece of shit couldn't just let him be. He just took him from me," I said as tears watered my eyes.

"It's okay, Nikki. We'll get through this together. Maybe I can ask Jayson to look into this Malachi and see what he can turn up."

"No. Janelle, I got you involved with Damien's psycho ass and he almost raped you. I'm not gonna get you twisted up with this nigga too. This is not your problem."

"Nikki, I'm a big girl now, and I know what you went through with Damien. I won't let you go through it again with anybody else." Janelle still thought it was her fault that Damien and Horse nearly beat me to death three years ago. It was my own reckless lifestyle that put me in that situation in the first place. I wouldn't put Janelle in harm's way again.

"Don't worry, Janelle. I'll be fine. Just don't tell Jayson about this. Malachi will get what he's got coming sooner or later. They always do. For now my only concern is Dre's health and raising Tyler. I just don't want him to grow up without his father."

"He's gonna pull out of this, Nikki. I know it."

I wished I could be so sure of that. It had been over a month since Dre slipped into this coma, and the doctors had no clue when he might come out of it, if he ever did. I had to be realistic about it. Dre might never wake up.

God, you can't do this to us. We've gone through so much already. We both changed so much, just to have our past come in and bite us in the ass. Please, God, just help my family.

***

The next morning, I dropped Tyler off at the daycare and headed to the hospital. As I was driving down Peachtree Street past the Fox Theater, I saw a black Escalade two cars behind me. I thought it was the same one I had seen in the parking garage the day before. It was following me. I knew I was not being paranoid now.

Who is it? Is it Malachi? Is he keeping tabs on me? Or is he trying to finish the job he started and kill Dre?

I pulled my car into a parking lot quickly, and the Escalade drove by. I looked through my rearview mirror and saw the guy behind the wheel. Same 24-inch rims I saw the day before. The tinted windows were down, and I got a real good look at his face. I had never seen him before, but I knew a dope boy when I saw one. He must have worked for Malachi. He wasn't going to let this go until Dre was dead. What was I gonna do now?

JASMINE

Some folks might have called me materialistic, money hungry, or superficial, and you know what? They were absolutely right! Fuck a dollar and a dream! I needed hundred dollar bills to make me cream!

I had The Pink Palace on lock. Plus I had Malachi breaking me off extra for the exclusive favors I gave him. With Malachi giving me top billing, I could afford to live a lavish life in a luxury condo in Buckhead, furnished with top of the line Italian furniture, contemporary appliances and fixtures, including a washer and dryer, not to mention a private indoor pool and private parking lot!

Like I said before, I was not your average stripper shaking my ass at a hole in the wall club. Before you think I was just another black girl lost from a broken home with daddy issues, I'll have you know I grew up with both of my parents in the house, and I graduated from Spelman College with a bachelors and masters of science degree. I started dancing at the Red Light Club to help me pay tuition. After finishing school and seeing how much money I was making a night from dancing, I decided not to take an internship getting coffee for some jackass in a suit.

But what set me apart from the average chick in the club was more than my pretty face, big boobs, bubbly personality, and voluptuous ass. It was my ambition. I didn't get caught up in the stripper lifestyle. This was a business, and I was all about my business! I had my own Web site, Facebook, and Twitter. I had over 25,000 followers on Twitter and Facebook, where I sold my own calendar with photos I had taken by Marian Designs in Atlanta. I also did private parties and traveled around the country to other clubs to dance for the right price: everywhere from Magic City, Sue's Rendezvous, The Rollexxx Club, and Erotic City. I got money!

I had no regrets—well, as far as my career choice. None. But I wished I never lost the friendship of my girls, Rashida and Joyce. Especially Rashida. I loved her. Let's just say things ended badly. I still had the lumps to prove it. But fuck it, that was the past. Money over niggas and bitches was my creed now, and as long as I had Malachi's nose wide open, my cash flow was unlimited.

I drove to The Pink Palace in my silver CLS550 Mercedes-Benz, and once I got inside, I saw my new plaything, Kandi. She was in the locker room, looking in the mirror, putting on her makeup. She was a cutie pie with that satin lace flyaway babydoll. Her fat little camel toe was imprinting through her matching satin panties. Just looking at her made me wet.

"Hey, Kandi," I said to her as I walked up behind her.

"Hey, Jasmine," she replied in a perky tone.

"You getting ready to hit the stage?"

"Yeah. I hope I can make a little extra money tonight," she confirmed as she finished applying her pink MAC lipstick.

"How come?" I asked.

"I just got some bills I need to catch up on."

"Your boyfriend can't help you out?"

"I don't have a boyfriend now," Kandi said and turned around and looked at me. "Well, at least not anymore."

"What happened?"

"He couldn't deal with me working here. Thinks I'm fucking every nigga in the club! So stupid. This is just a job."

"I hear ya. Men can be so damn insecure," I cosigned and caressed her arm. Um, I could tell she didn't mind my touch. That was always a good sign. "Listen, if you wanna make a little extra cash, I can hook you up."

"Really?"

"Yeah, I do a few private shows around town, and I can take you with me. The money is good, and the niggas are usually corporate types. Pushovers. Show 'em a little ass, let 'em touch a titty, and you'll get paid. If you up for it, just let me know."

"Am I? Hell yeah! I'm trying to get this money. Good looking out, Jasmine," she said and hugged me. "Ya know, at first I was a little nervous here, not knowing anybody, but you really be looking out for me. Thank you."

"It ain't nothing but a thing. I'll let you know when my next gig is."

"Cool. I better get on stage now. Talk to you later," Kandi said and walked to the stage.

Oh, sweet Kandi. I'ma take very good care of you all right.

I turned and looked in the mirror and smiled. I walked to the side of the stage and watched Kandi on stage doing her thing on the pole. The way she did them splits made me eager to get in between them thighs.

As I was watching the show, I saw a sexy-ass chocolate sista walk up in the club. Seeing a chick up in the club was nothing new. They were some of my best tippers. She was rockin' a V-neck blue Versace blouse, Seven jeans that looked like they were painted on that fat ass, and black Steve Madden stilettos. But this chick wasn't here for the show. She made her way to the stairs leading to Malachi's office. No way the security was gonna let her up to Malachi's office no matter how good she looked.

What the fuck? They just let her go up. That's not Malachi's wife. Who is she?

3

Dining With the Devil

Atlanta, GA

MALACHI

"I checked up on that job you had Reggie do," Ricky said as he sat in front of me. Ricky had been my right hand man for about ten years now. He'd been my most reliable soldier in the game.

"And?"

"Well, I found out that nigga Dre is up in Emory in a coma."

"A coma?"

"Yep. Looks like Reggie didn't quite get the job done like he thought," Ricky quipped as he was checking his iPhone.

"Damn. I swear that nigga can't piss straight without making a mess," I grumbled as I looked out the window at Reggie sitting at a table, getting a dance from a girl.

As I was looking at my retarded little brother, I saw the most stunning woman I'd seen in a while walk in the club. I saw ass every day, and I could fuck any bitch in there I wanted, so I was not easily impressed with too many women I see. But this one got my attention immediately. She walked through the club with confidence, and she seemed to have a glow about her. She was flawless.

"Who is that?" I asked Ricky, and he stood up and looked at her through the window.

"That's the chick I was following around in Dre's car. I think that's his girl. She's heading straight up here. Do you want me to tell security to keep her there?"

"No. Let her come up." Damn, this woman looked good. No wonder Dre decided to get out of the game. If she was brave enough to come here, then the least I could do was meet her.

Ricky made a call to security, and they let her up. Bump opened the door and let her in.

She was even more breathtaking up close. The look in her eyes was of disdain for me. For some reason, that aroused me even more. She cut her eyes to Ricky, as if telling him she knew he had been following her. Then she refocused her eyes on me. If security hadn't patted her down, she maybe would have brought a gun up there to kill me. Most folks showed fear around me, but not her.

"You wanted to see me?" I asked as I leaned back in my chair and looked at her lovely body before me. Her thickness in them jeans was astonishing.

"Malachi Turner," she said in a smooth, even tone. "I believe we have a mutual acquaintance in common."

"That might be so, but who, may I ask, are you?"

"My name is Nikki Bell. You've done business with my baby's father, Dre," she said proudly.

Hmmm . . . not too many women would walk into the lion's den for a nigga like this.

"What can I do for you, Ms. Bell?"

"I need for you to leave him alone. He's no threat to you or your business."

I smiled at the beautiful woman brave enough to speak to me so boldly, "Dre was never a threat to my business, but there was a matter of a debt he owed me."

"A debt he had paid in full."

"His debt isn't paid until I say it is," I coldly said to her.

She exhaled deeply and then glanced at Ricky, eyeing him like a shark. If looks could kill, Ricky would be done.

"Then I wanna know what I need to give you in order to settle it."

No fear. I'd rarely come across a woman with this kind of determination since I left Kingston years ago. She intrigued me.

"Ricky, give us a moment alone."

Ricky nodded at me and then gave Nikki another lustful glare before he left the room.

"Have a seat."

"I'd rather stand," she insisted, but there was only so much willfulness I would allow in my world. I was a god there.

"I said sit," I said in a more powerful tone.

She reluctantly obeyed.

I got up and walked around my desk and stood in front of her. Her luscious breasts rose and fell with each deep breath she took. The look on her face was steady, still no fear.

"What can you give me that I don't already have, Nikki?"

"What do you want? I can give you money, but you don't look like a man who needs the few dollars I can give you. Dre is the father of my son, Malachi. I don't want my son to grow up without his father in his life. As a man, you can understand what that can do to a boy," she said sincerely. "That's all he has. Don't take that away from him. Please?"

No one had ever appealled to me like that. A woman like that was who I could see with a nigga like me. I could have fucked her, but she would never really give herself to me . . . not at first. No, a woman like that had to be broken before she would give in. Materialistic things didn't seem to move her like most of the bitches in there. Most women would come in there with their pussy in my face, but not her.

"He's in a coma. No telling if he will ever wake up—if he's *allowed* to at all."

"I know. Don't take him away from us."

"Perhaps we can come to some kind of agreement. Maybe we can discuss this further over a nice meal?"

She looked at me inquisitively, as if weighing her options. "A meal? With me?"

"Yes. Dinner. You do eat?"

She had expected me to ask her for something else.

"Yes, of course. When?"

"Tomorrow night. I'll send a car for you, say around eight?"

"What about Dre?"

"He'll be fine. We'll discus his future as well," I said and extended my hand to her. She looked at it then took it and stood up.

I kissed her hand, and a sweet smell of cherries filled my nostrils. My dick started to rise in my boxers. She gently pulled her hand away.

"That's fine," she said and turned and walked to the door. Her ample ass bounced with every step. My dick wanted her ass right then. She opened the door and turned and looked at me one last time before exiting my office.

A few seconds passed, and Ricky came back inside.

"Damn, Malachi, I know what you're gonna do with all that ass right there."

"I want you to keep tabs on her. I wanna know her every move. You can never be too sure what a woman can be up to."

"Consider it done," Ricky said and left.

I knew exactly what she had in mind. It had been a long time since I had a challenge walk through my doors.

NIKKI

That was the scariest Jamaican I'd ever seen in my life. I felt like my heart was about to jump out of my chest. I'd dealt with his type before, so I knew how to handle myself around him. I didn't tell Janelle or Penny I was going to do this, because I knew they would try to stop me, but if I didn't do this, I knew he'd kill Dre. His boy Ricky was the one following me around town. I knew he worked for Malachi.

Nothing much had changed since the last time I'd been up in The Pink Palace. Mostly new girls, but they all did the same old tricks on stage. Same horny-ass men up in there, a few of them I knew from my days there. They stared at me like I was brand new. Guess they were not used to seeing me with my clothes on.

As I walked through the club, I did spot this one girl staring at me from the bar. She must have thought I was there to audition for a job. Never again.

I was prepared to do anything to convince Malachi not to hurt Dre. I knew that sex would most likely be my only option, but he had surprised me. He wanted to take me out to dinner. He must have wanted to get a full stomach before we fucked. Whatever. As long as he left Dre alone, I was willing to do whatever he wanted.

I got to my car and took off. I turned down Spring Street and entered I-75/85 and headed to College Park.

***

Today I was at the shop with Penny. I was still replaying the last night's events in my head, trying to figure if there was something else I could've done. Penny was putting some clothes back on the rack as I was sitting behind the counter in deep thought.

"What are you thinking about?" Penny asked me as she put the Averix hoodies on display.

"Nothing."

"Nikki, you can't keep worrying about Dre. I know it's hard not to, but you can't dwell on it every second of the day."

"Penny, I need to tell you something, and it's gotta stay between us," I said to her. Penny had been my girl for years. We'd done all sorts of things together, from our time together dancing at The Pink Palace, doing private shows for niggas, and even a few threesomes. There wasn't nothing that would shock her. In some ways, she knew me better than anybody else, so I knew she'd understand what I was going to tell her.

"You already know. What's up?"

"I went to The Pink Palace to see Malachi," I told her, and she stopped and looked at me disapprovingly.

"And why would you go and do something like that for, Nikki?" Penny said to me, upset.

"Because the other day when I was leaving the hospital, I saw a dude in a black Escalade watching me. Then yesterday the same Escalade was following me around town. Something told me it was Malachi trying to find out what condition Dre was in, and when I went to club, I saw the same nigga in Malachi's office with him."

"Oh my God. What happened?"

"Malachi's a big, scary-ass Jamaican: powerful, arrogant, and a control freak. I just wanted to look him in the eye and see if I could reason with him. Say something, anything to convince him to leave Dre alone."

"Nikki, we both know niggas like Malachi only want one thing from women like us."

"I know. He had that look in his eye. I love Dre, but if it meant fucking that nigga to get him to back off, I was prepared to do that too," I said to her, and Penny understood. We both knew that the power of pussy was the ultimate bargaining commodity that we had.

Penny walked up to the counter in front of me. "So what happens now?" she asked.

"He wants to take me out to dinner. Can you keep Tyler for me tonight?"

"Yeah, no problem. I know you have to do what you have to do, Nikki, but I don't wanna see you get hurt either. I don't think I could stand to see another man hurt you like that again," Penny said and took my hand. Penny had stood by my side while I recovered from the abuse Damien put me through years ago.

"That's not going to happen to me again. I'm not playing games like that anymore. I got too much to lose this time around."

I started getting dressed about 7:15 for my dinner date with Malachi. I couldn't believe I was about to break bread with the nigga responsible for putting Dre in a coma—not to mention what else he may have had in mind for me. But it didn't matter. As long as Dre's life was at stake, I was willing to do anything to protect him.

I decided to wear a simple black D & G cocktail dress that showed plenty of legs, matching Prada high heels, and a silver necklace with a heart-shaped pendant. My hair was in an updo, with two Chinese sticks in the back. My MAC makeup was flawless, as I gave myself a once over in the mirror.

Eight o'clock sharp, a black stretch limo pulled in front of my house. Funny how Malachi knew where I lived already.

I walked outside, and the driver got out and opened my door for me. Malachi was trying to impress me.

Pretty soon, we drove down Old National Highway and got on I-85 North to Midtown Atlanta. My only thoughts were what did I have to do to get Malachi to leave Dre alone.

The driver exited off 248B and then turned down Peachtree Street, and we soon pulled in front of The Melting Pot fondue restaurant. The driver let me out, and I walked to the door and went inside. It was a dimly lit restaurant that was sectioned off for a more intimate feel.

The hostess behind the podium smiled at me. "Hello. Welcome to The Melting Pot. Do you have a reservation?"

"Yes, I think it's made out to Malachi Turner?"

She looked over her guest book. "Yes, please come with me."

She escorted me through the restaurant, and we passed by the glass wall with what looked like a hundred bottles of wine on the wall, then around the corner down a passageway past the bar. Then she turned another corner and led me to a booth in the back, where I saw Malachi sitting at the table waiting for me.

He stood up and smiled as he looked me up and down. "Hello, Nikki," he said in a deep Jamaican accent. He was dressed to the nines in a custom tailored tan suit and brown gators. He extruded the same confidence he had the other night.

"Hello, Malachi," I said as I took a seat.

"Your server will be with you in a moment," the hostess said and walked away. I tried to calm my nerves as I looked at the menu.

"You look exquisite tonight, Nikki," Malachi said to me.

"Thank you."

"I'm glad you decided to come dine with me tonight."

"I didn't have much of a choice," I said as I tried to hold back my discontent with the thought of eating with him.

"Of course you had a choice, and you chose to be here with me tonight."

"Nice restaurant," I said, trying to change the subject.

"Yes, it's one of my favorite places to eat. I know you'll enjoy the cuisine."

To my surprise, I did enjoy the fondue shrimp and steak. I was surprised at how fast and delicious the meat was cooked in the small fondue pot on the table in front of us.

For the most part, Malachi talked about himself. Like most egomaniacs, he enjoyed the sound of his own voice. He told me about leaving Jamaica when he was fifteen years old and his rise to power here in Atlanta. Surprisingly enough, he had bought The Pink Palace just a few months after I quit working there. I wondered if he knew that I did dance there.

Then he flipped the conversation to me.

"So how old is your son?"

I paused for a moment, unsure if I wanted to talk about Tyler with him. "He'll be two in March."

"What's his name?" Malachi asked.

"Tyler."

"Good name."

"Yes, his father gave him it," I said, and Malachi smirked.

"I can see you're a woman very loyal to your man."

"That's the only reason why I'm here."

"No, it's not. There is a number of ways you could've handled this situation."

I put my fork down and glared at him. "You gave me no choice. You were going to kill Dre."

"I never said that to you. I just merely asked you out to dinner."

"Then why did you have your boy Ricky following me around at the hospital?"

"I wanted to have an update on Dre's situation. If you thought I was going to harm him, you could've went to the police," Malachi said then took another bite of his steak.

I wanted to grab a knife and stab him in the eyes for what he did to Dre.

"But you didn't. You chose to come to me. You chose to come to dinner with me tonight because I'm the type of nigga a woman like you wants."

Muthafucka. In some ways he was right. Back in the day, I would've been all up on him, doing whatever and taking his money. But I was not that woman anymore. Not after what I'd been through.

"The only thing I want is for you to leave Dre alone. I'm here willing to do whatever it takes to make that happen. If sex is what you want, then let's just get to that and stop all this wining and dining shit."

"Finish your food," Malachi said and just continued to eat his food as if he didn't hear me. Arrogant son of a bitch.

4

Sexual Seduction

Buckhead, GA

JASMINE

"I'll come pick you up from the club around ten," I said to Kandi over the phone.

"That'll be good. Thanks for hooking me up with this party, Jasmine!"

"Like I said, it's no problem. Just be ready to make this money."

"I'm ready for whatever! I'll see you in a few," Kandi replied, and I hung up.

Hmmm, ready for whatever, huh? We'll see, young Kandi, we'll see.

I looked myself over in the mirror. I was wearing a gray V-neck Elizabeth and James cardigan with a black lace bra underneath. The cardigan hung on my body like a mini-skirt, showing off my long, thick legs, and I had on gray python-printed Christian Louboutin pumps. I wore two silver Cuban link chains with a cross on one and a Hello Kitty charm on the other. My hair was down, parted in the middle, looking good after my trip to Alres Salon and Spa. My makeup was flawless as usual. I was the shit!

I jumped in my silver CLS550 Mercedes-Benz and headed to The Pink Palace. I decided to go through the city and down Peachtree Street. I was blasting Lil' Wayne's "Lollipop" as I cruised down the street. Sweet Kandi was definitely gonna be my lollipop tonight!

As I got closer to the club, I stopped at a red light and saw a limo outside of The Melting Pot restaurant, and then I saw Malachi and that chick I saw at the club the other night coming out. Who the hell was she? I had to admit that she looked cute in her black D & G cocktail dress. Bitch had style. But how did she get so close to Malachi so quickly? Something was going on.

The light changed green, and I pulled off and headed to The Pink Palace.

I got to the club and saw Kandi standing out front, waiting for me. She had on a white tube top and mini-skirt with black stilettos. Hmmm, I was going to have to step her fashion game up in the future.

I pulled up to the curb, and she opened the door and jumped in.

"Hey, Jasmine! Girl, I couldn't wait for you to get here."

"I see. Cute outfit you got on," I lied.

"This ain't nothing compared to what you got on. What did you do, raid Rihanna's closet? That shit is hot!"

"I just threw this together. I'll hook you up with some stuff later if you like."

"Hell yeah! Jasmine, you my girl. So where is this party at?" Kandi asked as I turned on to I-20 West.

"It's out in Lithonia. Some local rapper called Young Reezy wants me to entertain them tonight. You know how the young niggas with record deals spend cash!"

"Yeah, he's got that song called 'Booty Butterfly.' When you say entertain them, you mean just dancing, right?" Kandi asked nervously.

"I'ma be real with you, Kandi. If you wanna get down with Young Reezy, that's on you. Personally, his paper ain't long enough for me to give him some pussy. We're just going there and doing our thing and get paid, all right?"

"That sounds good to me."

About twenty minutes later, we pulled into a private neighborhood in Lithonia. There were about thirty cars parked in front of a big house, almost like a mini mansion. Kandi and I parked and walked up to the front door and rang the bell. Music was blasting from inside of the house. A few seconds later the door opened.

"Oh, shit," a young nigga said as he looked us up and down. He had on a long white tee, baggy black jeans, and a red A-town hat.

"We're tonight's entertainment," I told him, and he let us in. The house was full of niggas, with a few chicks here and there.

I scanned the room and saw Young Reezy sitting in the center of a long, L-shaped sofa, surrounded by groupies and his entourage. Young Reezy was iced out, with four platinum chains, diamond-encrusted brace-lets around each wrist, and a diamond-encrusted grill in his mouth. I swear those rappers didn't know what to do with their money. He glanced over and smiled then nodded his head.

"Can you take us to a room so we can change?" I said to the young nigga that let us in. His eyes were glued on my ass.

"Uh, yeah. Dis way," he said and took us to a back room down a long hallway. The room had a big bed and a 42-inch plasma hanging on the wall that was hooked up to a PS3. The dresser had a bunch of games and a collection of porn on it. The boom-boom room, no doubt.

The dude that let us in was still standing at the door, ogling us.

"Where's my money?"

"Huh?"

"Money, nigga! We needs to get paid before anything pops off," I said to him as I looked him up and down.

"Yeah, I got ya," he said, and he went out to the party.

I turned and looked at Kandi.

"Always get your money first. No cash, then you don't see no ass."

"I know that's right," Kandi said as she sat on the bed.

The dude came back with an envelope and gave it to me. I counted the cash, and it was ten thousand in hundred-dollar bills as agreed.

The dude was once again staring at us.

"You can leave now," I said and closed the door on him. I counted out three thousand and gave it to Kandi. "Here you go, girl."

"Damn, Young Reezy is ballin', huh?" Kandi asked me.

"Kandi, don't be sucked in by this. This ain't real money. This dude got a little paper. This is just some nigga spending all his advance money on bullshit. Trust me, if you stick with me, I'll show you the niggas with cash."

She nodded and then went into her bag and pulled out a bikini then started to undress. Her body was curvy and tight. Her ass was round and fat, and I felt myself getting wet looking at her.

Kandi turned and looked at me. "Aren't you gonna change?"

"Yeah." She had no idea.

I pulled off my cardigan and noticed that Kandi was looking at me too. I looked up at her and smiled, and she smiled back nervously and continued to get dressed.

I changed into my black panties with the furry balls hanging from it, and slipped on my black high heel Prada shoes. A few minutes later, we came out of the room and walked back out to the living room, and all eyes were on us. Niggas were drooling, and bitches were turning up their noses and hating, mad that they didn't look as good as us.

"Who's Young Reezy?" I yelled as if I didn't know, and he smiled.

"That's me," he said, and I gestured with my finger for him to come to me. His niggas started to squeal and yell as I called him out.

He got up and came to the center of the room.

"So you the one that made that song 'Booty Butterfly'?"

"Yeah," he said and smiled.

"What you know about that?" I said as I traced my fingers over his chest and down to his crotch.

"I know what I know."

"Well, let me show you what a real booty butterfly is," I said, and Kandi grabbed a chair behind him. I pushed him back into it. "Play that shit!"

The DJ started the song. *Booty Butterfly, Booty Butterfly, make ya ass cheeks flap like a butterfly. Booty Butterfly, Booty Butterfly, make ya ass cheeks flap like a butterfly.*

I bent over and started to make my ass clap in his face. Kandi joined me, and the niggas went wild. Reezy started to smack our asses softly, and I decided to give him a ride. I sat in his lap and gyrated my ass, and I could feel his hard dick through his jeans.

Kandi started to dance for some other niggas, and they started tipping her.

"Oh, shit!" Young Reezy yelled.

I loved making niggas excited. "You like my butter-fly?"

"Hell yeah, shit! I like both of y'all butterfly!"

"You do? Kandi, Reezy likes your booty butterfly too," I yelled at her, and she strutted over to us. She bent over and started to clap her ass for him, while I was riding. I got up, and then Kandi straddled him cowgirl style in the chair.

"Yeah!" Reezy yelled.

"Let's take this to the next level," I said and slid up behind Kandi so we were both on Reezy, and then I slid my hand down Kandi's stomach and underneath her bikini.

"What are you doing?" Kandi asked me.

"Just go with it. Trust me," I whispered in her ear.

"I don't know. . . . Ah . . ."

My fingers found Kandi's clit before she could pro-test any further. I gave Young Reezy an up-close view of me playing with Kandi's pussy.

"This is off the chain," Reezy yelled as he fondled Kandi's titties.

I began to kiss Kandi on her neck as I continued to fondle her. Her pussy got so wet. Before she knew it, Kandi was having an orgasm right in front of us.

"Oh, shit!" Kandi cried out and came.

I pulled my fingers out from under her bikini and turned her face and kissed her. She kissed me back as I darted my tongue in and out of her mouth.

Pretty soon we forgot Young Reezy was the one we were supposed to be entertaining. He was just enjoying the show at this point.

I pulled away and got up off of Reezy, and Kandi gave me a look of shock. I smiled then turned my attention to some of the other niggas in the room. After a twenty-minute show, we both headed back to the bedroom in the back.

I closed and locked the door behind us.

Kandi was noticeably quiet.

"You good, girl?" I asked her as I counted the tips I had made.

"Yeah . . . Jasmine," Kandi said nervously and sat on the bed.

"What's up?"

"About what happened out there. . . . Ah, I'm not gay. I mean, I like men," Kandi said, still in shock.

"Okay, so do I. I like you too. You never kiss a girl before?" I asked her and sat next to her on the bed.

"Yeah, I have, but nothing like what you did to me."

I grinned. "Did you like it?"

"What?" Kandi said, taken off guard by my question.

"You heard me. I know you did. That kiss wasn't just one way," I said and caressed her thigh.

Kandi bit her bottom lip as I moved my hand back up to her crotch.

"It felt good, didn't it?"

Kandi nodded her head as I rubbed her clit through her thong.

"You want me to make you cum again, Kandi?"

"Yes . . . no, I'm not . . . gay."

"Kandi, haven't you ever been curious about it?" I said then kissed her. A soft moan escaped her lips, and I pushed her back on the bed. I pulled down her thong, and her coochie was nice and creamy. I took off her thong and spread her thick, chocolate legs and licked her swollen clit. Kandi moaned, and I continued to lick her slowly. She tasted just as sweet as I thought she would.

5

Deal with the Devil

Atlanta, GA

MALACHI

She was a beautiful thing, even when she was upset. Since we left the restaurant, she hadn't said anything else to me as we rode up Peachtree Road in the limo to the Ritz Carlton. She stared out the window as I sat across from her, drinking my Courvoisier. She kept insisting she loved Dre, but she was there with me? I knew that deep down inside she really loved power.

That was what I represented: power. And as much as she may not have wanted to admit it, she was drawn to me. A woman like Nikki wanted a nigga like me in her life. She just didn't know it yet.

We got to the Ritz and checked into a penthouse suite overlooking Lenox Mall. Still no words were exchanged between us. She walked to the mini bar, took a mini-bottle of Smiroff vodka, and downed it. Then she looked at me blankly, turned, and walked to the bedroom.

I took off my jacket and tossed it into a chair and followed behind her.

I walked in and Nikki was standing by the bed. She reached up and pulled the strap of her dress over her right shoulder. Then she pulled down the left strap, and her dress fell to the ground. Her body was flawless in her black lace bra and panties.

I walked around her and kissed her on the neck, then I unclasped her bra and it fell to the ground. Then I caressed her breasts with both hands. Her nipples became hard along with my dick.

I laid her on the bed and pulled her panties off. Then I spread her long, luscious legs, exposing her fat pussy. I used my tongue and tasted her sweet nectar.

She tried to fight the feeling, but I could tell her body couldn't deny it by how wet she was getting. I licked her clit from left to right, slurping her juices.

She stifled a moan and gripped the sheets, still fighting the sensations I was giving her.

"You like it, don't you?" I asked her, but she didn't answer. "I know you do, Nikki. I know you do." I licked her faster.

She tried to pull away, but I gripped her legs. I swirled my tongue around her walls. She came in my mouth, and her arms flayed on the bed as her body jerked involuntarily until she couldn't hold back anymore.

"Oh, shit. Ah, ah, shit," Nikki moaned.

I stood up and unbuckled my belt and pulled down my slacks and boxers. My dick stood long and hard.

Nikki was still trying to recover from her orgasm as she lay spread eagle on the king-size bed. I rubbed my shaft with her moistness then climbed on top of her. I grabbed her face and made her look at me. Then I kissed her.

She tried to resist, but I wouldn't let her move. Then I pushed my long, hard rod inside her wetness. Damn, she felt so good.

She turned her head to the side and closed her eyes as I stroked her hard and deep.

"Look at me," I said as I continued to stroke her. She ignored me. "Look at me!"

She reluctantly obeyed and looked me in the eyes,

"This is my pussy," I asserted and gave her a hard, deep stroke. "Whose pussy is this?"

She frowned and bit her bottom lip. "Yours."

I smiled and continued to have my way with her for the rest of the night. That pussy belonged to me from now on.

NIKKI

I woke up in bed, sore from the sex I'd had with Malachi. I felt so angry with myself for being with him, and even more disgusted for enjoying some of it. I hated myself. But I did what I had to for Dre.

I heard Malachi in the bathroom. I just wanted to grab my clothes and leave, but I couldn't leave yet. I wrapped the sheet around me and got up out of the bed. I needed to shower and wash his funk off of me.

The bathroom door opened, and Malachi stood there in his boxers, grinning at me.

"Good morning, my dear."

I glared at him and didn't answer.

"You were magnificent last night, Nikki."

"I'm glad you enjoyed yourself," I retorted sarcastically.

"Oh, I did, and I wasn't the only one that did."

"Whatever, Malachi. We're done with each other," I affirmed and started to walk to the bathroom.

"I thought you said you wanted to make a deal regarding Dre?"

I paused and turned around, "What's there to discuss? We fucked! You got what you wanted from me. What more do you want?"

"That wasn't a deal, Nikki. That was sex. What I want from you is much more profitable."

I was standing there in shock. What the hell did this nigga want from me?

"What are you talking about?"

"My dear Nikki, I want you to be my number one dancer. I want you at The Pink Palace."

"What? I'm not gonna dance there," I yelled, pissed the fuck off.

Malachi smiled. "You did before."

"How did you know that? What does this have to do with Dre?"

"Dre is in a coma. The doctors don't know if he'll ever wake up, so he might as well be dead. You are just too lovely to let get away. Besides, it'll be like a homecoming for you, right? I did a little research on you, and you were the club's number one draw back in the day. You can help Dre settle his debt with me."

"You're out of your damn mind. I won't do it."

"If you want Dre to stay alive you will. You'll be at The Pink Palace Friday night, ready to work." Malachi walked up to me and pulled my sheet away. "Yes, you'll definitely be my number one girl. The limo will be waiting for you downstairs when you're done. Don't worry, Nikki. I'm gonna take very good care of you."

I couldn't believe that shit! How had I let this happen to me again?

Malachi kissed my lips then turned and picked up his clothes and started to get dressed. I walked into the bathroom, locked the door behind me, and got in the shower. Tears streamed down my face as the hot water washed over me.

He would kill Dre if I refused to go back. There was no other option for me. I had worked so hard to get away from that life, and now I had no choice but to do it again.

I made sure to stay in the shower extra long. When I came out of the bathroom, Malachi was gone. My dress was laid out on the bed, and on top of it were five one hundred–dollar bills. He left the cash behind like I was a prostitute.

Tears watered my eyes as anger filled my heart. I knocked the bills on the ground and got dressed. I went downstairs and saw a limo out front, waiting for me. I didn't want to take it, but I didn't have any other choice on how to get home.

After I got home, I changed clothes and headed to Emory to see Dre. When I got there, he was still in a coma. Half of me always hoped to see him up and waiting for me to come in. Instead, I walked in and sat by his side and took his hand.

"I'm so sorry, Dre," I said as I rubbed his hand. "I thought . . . I thought I could protect you."

Dre looked so peaceful.

Please wake up. Just open your eyes for me.

I thought of our son, and I didn't want him to grow up without a father. I didn't want him to go down the same path so many young black boys had traveled without a father figure. What kind of example could I set for him dancing at The Pink Palace?

Just as I was lost in thought about our son's future, the door opened and a black female walked in. She was quite beautiful and young.

"Hello, Ms. Bell," she said to me.

"Yes."

"My name is Dr. Griffin," she said and shook my hand.

I looked at her badge and read Dr. Nia Griffin. I didn't see too many black females as doctors around there.

"I'll be Andre's new doctor."

"Oh, okay. How is he doing?"

She began to look over his chart and checked his vitals. "He's stable, and that's the good news. Ms. Bell . . ."

"You can call me Nikki."

"Nikki, his body is healing itself. We really don't know how long this coma will last. He could wake up tomorrow for all we know."

"Or he could die," I said to her.

"Yes, but I'm gonna do my best to prevent that. I'm going to give you some more time with him," Dr. Scott said and left the room.

I believed she would do everything she could for Dre, just like I planned to do everything I could to protect him.

6

Ego

Atlanta, GA

JASMINE

Another Friday night at The Pink Palace, so it was time for me to get that money. I parked and came in through the employee entrance in the back that led to the locker rooms. I got there late, but when you were the number one money-getter, you were always on time.

I saw Kandi looking at herself in the mirror, adjusting her red baby doll teddy, looking like a sexy Bratz doll. I hadn't seen her since the night we hooked up at Young Reezy's party.

She spotted my reflection in the mirror and gave me a shy smile. She turned around and walked over to me at my dressing table.

"What's up, Jasmine?" Kandi crooned.

I smiled at her. "What's up you? You look cute."

"Thanks. I took some of that money I made at the party and bought myself some new outfits."

"Good. 'Cause some of that other shit you was wearing before wasn't cutting it," I informed her.

"Oh." Kandi looked at me oddly. "Jasmine, about what happen at the party . . ."

I grinned at her seductively, "We had fun."

"I know . . . but I'm not gay," she whispered so some of the other girls wouldn't hear.

I turned around and looked at her. "Kandi, I know you're not gay. Neither am I. I love me some dick, but every now and then, I like to taste something sweet. Besides, by the way you were moaning, you didn't seem to be to worry about being gay or not."

Kandi blushed. "I know, but . . ."

"But what?" I retorted and looked at her straightforwardly. "We fucked. No big deal. You're young, sexy, and having fun. Besides, when was the last time your man made you feel that good?"

"Not in a long time," she said modestly.

"So there! I ain't trying to turn you out or make you my bitch," I explained with a laugh. She giggled too. "You're going to have to lighten up, girl!"

"Okay, so do you have any more private parties we can do?"

"I'll let you know," I said and gave her a wink.

I knew I could have her ass anytime I wanted now. It was always good to have a young tenderoni in your pocket. "So what's been going on here?"

"Well, some new chick just started here tonight."

I rolled my eyes. "Another newbie? Great. I hope she stays away from Reggie's horny ass."

"Ah, I don't think she's a newbie," Kandi told me. "Malachi brought her in himself, and a lot of the niggas up in here been going crazy for her."

I narrowed my eyes at her. "You said Malachi brought her up in here himself?"

"Yep. He was giving her the royal treatment and shit. She must be something special," Kandi noted.

I didn't like that shit at all. If any bitch in there should have been getting the royal treatment from

Malachi, it should have been me! I'd worked too hard to become the number one moneymaker there to be upstaged by some random bitch Malachi decided to bring in.

"Where is this trick?"

Kandi pointed toward the stage. "This is her third encore dance since she's been here. Niggas are wildin' out over her."

"What!" I fumed and walked to the stage. I saw this chick on stage, swinging on the pole like a triathlon! She was good. Ludacris's "How Low" song was blasting, and she dropped into a split and made her ass bounce as niggas were throwing money at her left and right. Sure, there were plenty of hoes there who could do the same thing, but none of them had a body like that.

Then I saw her face. It was the same chick that was out to dinner with Malachi the other night!

"Who is this bitch?" I mumbled.

"They call her Nikki," Kandi informed me.

What the hell was Malachi doing? He had never taken me out to eat or anything! What was so special about her? Who was she really? Obviously by the way she moved she wasn't no newbie. Maybe she was from out of town and Malachi brought her in to make some more money.

I had to admit that this Nikki was a sexy-looking bitch with long, chocolate legs, a fat, round ass, and a flawless face. I watched her for another few minutes until her set was over, and I went back to the locker room. I was gonna have to see what was up with her.

NIKKI

It was like riding a bike, dancing on that stage again. My mind went on autopilot, and my body fell back into the same old freaky gyrations and motions I used to do there three years ago. Malachi decided to bring me up in there himself and hyped up my return to The Pink Palace. I couldn't stand his ass for blackmailing me back into this shithole!

As I was walking off stage, I felt a strong pair of hands grab my arm and pull me toward him. I knew some nigga ain't had the nerve to put his got-damn hands on me! I may have been gone for a while, but not long enough for me not to bust a nigga upside the head!

"What are you doing here?"

I looked at his face and it was Polo, Dre's best friend. Polo's real name was Teddy Williams. He had been Dre's best friend since grade school. After Dre got out of the game, Polo had taken over his spots for him. Polo was tall and muscular, six foot two brother, with butterscotch-tone skin. He was lucky I knew him, or a Budweiser bottle would have been going over his head.

I yanked my arm away from him. "Polo, why you grabbing me like that, and what are you doing here?"

"I asked you first."

I rolled my eyes. "What does it look like?"

"Nikki, what the hell are you doing here? Dre's in the hospital fighting for his life, and you're up in here shaking your ass for the nigga who put him in there," Polo growled.

I sighed. "You don't understand."

"Then explain it to me!"

"I'm up in here beause I'm trying to keep Dre alive!"

Polo got a confused look on his face. "What?"

"Malachi is making me work off Dre's debt or he'll finish the job on Dre," I said through clenched teeth.

Polo shook his head. "Damn it. This is wrong. You can't do this, Nikki."

"I have no choice."

"I should've killed that nigga." Polo scowled.

I remembered just a few weeks ago, I was telling him to do that, but Polo was nowhere as deep as Malachi. He would be cut down before he could ever get close to him. Just him talking to me like that in the club could be dangerous for him. I knew Malachi must have been watching me.

"No. Listen, Polo, I gotta do this. I got this under control. Stay out of it. I have to go."

"Nikki, you'll never pay back that much money."

"I don't have any choice," I told him and walked back to the lockers. I had to get away from him before Malachi started asking who he was to me and found out his connection to Dre. I didn't need another person I knew hurt by Malachi.

As I walked into the locker room, a lot of the girls gave me the stink eye. A few I recognized; most I didn't. They didn't like the fact that I was back. Neither did I, but I had to do what I had to do.

This one chick standing across the room was smirking at me oddly. She was a pretty redbone with high cheekbones, big titties, and a small waist. I could tell right away she was the head bitch at The Palace, the same way I was when I was there three years ago.

I pretended not to notice her staring at me and walked over to my locker. I started to count my money as she and some other little brown-skinned chick walked toward me. I tucked my money away in my bag and closed my locker.

"Hey, you look real good out there," the redbone chick said to me slyly.

"Thanks," I replied cautiously.

"Listen, they call me Jasmine. This here is Kandi."

I looked over to Kandi and she gave me a blank stare.

"I'm Nikki."

"Well, Nikki, I see you've made quite the first impression out there, but you should know I'm the queen bitch here at The Pink Palace, so any thoughts you might be having about coming up in here and taking over, you can forget it."

I rolled my eyes. "Well, Queen Bee, you can relax. I'm only here to get this paper. You can have the groupies. Most of the guys here know me and know how I get down."

She squinted her eyes. "Know you? You've been here before?"

"Yeah, you can say that. Like I said, I'm only here for this paper." I walked away from them and headed back toward the exit.

"And Malachi?" Jasmine inquired.

I turned and stared at her. She must have been sucking his dick and thought I would take away her meal ticket. Fuck Malachi. She could have him. I turned back around and walked out of the lockers without another word.

7

Special Circumstances

Atlanta, GA

MALACHI

Watching Nikki on stage was almost as arousing as fucking her. Even though she wouldn't give herself to me completely, she was still exceptional. My dumb-ass brother Reggie was supposed to kill Dre, but instead put him in a coma, which brought Nikki's fine ass straight to me. I promised to let that nigga live if she came and worked for me, but if that nigga woke up, I'd kill him anyway. It was a win-win situation for me.

My iPhone rang and I answered the line. "Talk."

"We have a problem Malachi," Ricky informed me.

"I pay you to solve problems."

He swallowed hard. "I will, but you should know—"

"Not over the phone. Where are you?"

"At the spot."

"Come here now," I directed him.

"On my way." Ricky ended the call.

It must have been a situation if Ricky felt the need to call me. Another problem that I had to address, as if the fucking police weren't stressing me out enough. Good thing I had Detective Raymond on my payroll keeping the heat off me. Now if somebody could keep my damn baby mama Latoya out of my ass, things would be perfect. I swore if it weren't for my daughter, I would have made her dig a hole for herself.

I decided to smoke a blunt to relax my nerves when Bump called my line.

"What?"

"Jasmine wants to see you, boss," Bump replied.

"Send her in."

Bump opened the door, and Jasmine sashayed her sexy ass inside. Her ass was hanging out of her red boy shorts. Her big-ass titties looked nice and ripe, with her hard nipples protruding out of her bikini top. Jasmine was one sexy bitch. She sat her fat ass on my desk and pursed her lips together.

I leaned back in my chair. "What can I do for you, my dear?"

"You can tell me who that bitch is," Jasmine inquired, pointing out my window toward Nikki on the club floor. The jealously was obvious. Most girls in there couldn't really hold a candle to Jasmine, but Nikki was just as sexy.

"That's Nikki," I replied.

She frowned. "That much I know already. Why did you bring her up in here? I thought I was your number one girl."

"Nikki is here under special circumstances. Nothing you need to concern yourself with," I explained to her.

Jasmine folded her arms and glared at me. "So those *special circumstances* include dinner with you?"

I glared back at her. "Yes. You have a problem with that?"

Jasmine quickly realized that questioning what I did was not a wise thing to do.

"No . . . it's just . . . I was just curious as to why she's getting special treatment," she mumbled.

I stood up and caressed my fingers down the side of Jasmine's full breast. I tugged on her bikini top, making her titty pop out. My thumb ran over her hard nipple, and my dick grew harder.

She smiled and undid her bikini top, revealing her succulent breasts. She stood up, and I undid her shorts and pulled them down over her fat ass.

"Whatcha want, daddy?" she purred.

"You," I said and undid my pants and pulled out my black Anaconda. I stroked the beast and sat back down in my chair.

Jasmine turned around and sat her ass down in my lap, gently easing my massive dick into her wet pussy. Damn, she felt so fucking warm. She slid up and down my shaft like a stripper pole. She put her hands on my desk and wound her waistline round and round, pushing her ass back.

"Oh, shit, daddy. You feel so good," she crooned.

"Ride it. Yes, just like that, you sexy bitch," I moaned and slapped her ass.

"Ow, ah, ah . . ." Jasmine groaned as I grabbed her hips and worked my pipe up the middle of her wetness.

I gave her hard, fast strokes as I pushed her forward and stood behind her so I could get up in it further. I glanced back behind me through the club window and saw Nikki dancing and imagined it was her I was fucking again.

"Damn, Malachi, you fucking the shit outta me," Jasmine cried as I banged her back in.

The sound of my dick smacking her pussy filled my office. Her face was now down on top of my desk as I had her bent over. Feeling my nut coming, I withdrew from her pussy and spewed my seeds on her backside. I groaned deeply as I emptied my shaft. I wouldn't make the same mistake again, cumming inside one of those bitches and having another baby. That was how I got stuck with Latoya's ass in the first place.

"Go clean yourself up."

I tucked my dick back in my boxers and zipped up.

"Okay, baby . . . and uh . . ." She held out her hand. Just like a greedy bitch. Money was never too far off of her mind.

I reached in my pocket and took two Gs off of my money clip and tossed it on the desk. She scooped it up while she was still bent over my desk. She stood up and counted the money as my cum ran down the crack of her ass. She took some napkins off my desk and wiped her ass off then started to dress herself.

I sat back down in my chair, still enjoying the aftershocks of my orgasm. "So you're going to be at the grand opening of my new club next month?"

She grinned. "Of course. As long as I'm the headliner making top dollar."

"Of course," I confirmed.

"Good, 'cause you know I'm the best," she boasted. "And not some other chick."

I picked up my blunt and relit it. All those bitches thought their pussy was better than the next bitch. Too bad for her, Nikki's pussy was on my mind while I was fucking her.

"You can leave now."

Jasmine tucked her money in her bikini top and left my office. I turned in my chair and looked at Nikki again. I was going to have her ass again real soon.

Thirty minutes later, Ricky came up in the club and made his way to my office. He told me there was a problem over the phone, so he had better explain. Nobody had better be fucking up my money.

He walked in and had a seat in front of my desk.

"What the fuck is the problem?" I asked him.

"Jorge is dead."

"What?"

Ricky shook his head. "Yeah, Malachi, somebody wiped out Jorge and his whole crew and took our shit. They were five men deep, and they all got Swiss-cheesed up."

"Twenty kilos of coke gone! Fuck," I snapped. "Who's stupid enough to steal from me?"

"I don't know, but I'm already on it. I got mutha-fuckas on the streets checking shit out. One of these small-time niggas might be trying to grow some balls."

I looked Ricky in the eyes. "You better cut them fucking off."

JASMINE

Well, that didn't accomplish shit! Malachi wasn't saying shit about whatever this Nikki and he had going on. Instead, all he gave me was some stiff dick and a sore pussy. At least I got some cash for my services, but I was even more curious about what special circumstances Nikki had going on.

As I was walking down the stairs from Malachi's office, I spotted Reggie harassing some girls again. Hmmm. Malachi might not have wanted to tell me what's going on with Nikki, but I bet I could get dumb-ass Reggie to give me some info.

"What's up, Reggie?"

He turned and glared at me. "I ain't bothering nobody, Jasmine."

I smiled. "Did I say you were? I was just saying what's up."

"Oh, okay," Reggie replied, confused by my kindness.

"I see there's a new girl dancer here now. Calls herself Nikki. You know her?"

"Yeah. Nikki used to dance here a few years ago. Looks like she got thicker too! Her and this other chick—" Reggie thought about it for a moment. "This other chick called Mo'Nique used to trick up in here before they quit."

"You knew her back then?"

"Not really. I just used to come up in here and watch them hoes dance. Nikki used to fuck with all the big-time hustlers that used to come up in here. Why? You feeling a little intimidated by her?" Reggie said sarcastically.

I rolled my eyes. "Hell naw. I just wanted to know who she is."

Reggie picked up his beer and took a sip. "So, Jasmine, you gonna give me a dance at my birthday party next month?"

I eyed him up and down. "You know my fee. As long as the money is right, I might."

"Shit! I got that. How much more I gotta give you for a private dance that night?"

I cut my eyes at him. "What you trying to ask me, Reggie?"

"I know you fucking my brother, so I just wanna know how can I be down?"

"You can't afford me, nigga." I turned and walked away from his ugly behind. Besides, he had given me some more info I didn't know about this Nikki. So she used to dance there years ago, and now she was back. Why? What did Malachi have that she wanted?

8

Disappearing Act

College Park, GA

NIKKI

My body was so damn sore. I hadn't danced like that in over three years, and I wasn't as young as I used to be. I didn't get in until four in the morning. I'd been dancing at The Pink Palace all week. It was a good thing I had Penny working for me at the store because I didn't think I could have made it in that day even if I tried.

Seeing Polo at the club the other night had not helped at all. The look on his face when he saw me was total disgust. He was Dre's best friend, but he didn't realize I was doing this for Dre. Fucking Malachi was making me his dancing slave to spare Dre's life.

My iPhone started to play Alicia Keyes' "Try Sleeping With A Broken Heart," and I rolled over and looked at the display and saw Janelle's name. Shit. It was 8:10 a.m. and Janelle had Tyler for me the night before. Between her and Penny, they'd been helping me take care of him since Dre got hurt. I was supposed to pick him up so Janelle could get to work on time.

I pushed the button on my phone. "Janelle, I'm on my way, cuz. I overslept!"

"It's okay, Nikki. I'm off today," Janelle calmly replied.

"Oh. I feel like crap."

"How come? You're still not sleeping because of Dre?"

If only she knew. "Yeah, it's because of Dre."

"Tell you what, Nikki. Let's meet today for lunch at Taco Mac in midtown," Janelle suggested.

"Okay. About twelve thirty?"

"Sounds good. I'll bring Tyler."

"Thanks, Janelle. I don't know how I'll get through all this without you."

"Nikki, you were there for me when I needed you. I'll always be there for you. I'll see you later."

"All right, cuz." She hung up.

I put my hands over my face. *What have I gotten myself into?*

Two hours later, I rolled my ass out of bed and staggered to the shower. The warm water felt good over my sore muscles. I never used to feel like this back in the day. Of course, I was doing every other night, and that was pre-baby. I hadn't lost a step when it came to dancing, and I could still shake my ass with the best of them.

Only that Jasmine chick thought I was there to take her spot. Shit, she could have it. If this was the old me, I woulda been shut her ass down, but the only thing keeping me there was Malachi holding Dre's life over my head.

I'd been so caught up dancing at The Palace again that I hadn't had time to go check on Dre in the hospital. Look at me lying to myself. I hadn't gone to see Dre because I felt ashamed of doing that shit again, a life I swore to him I was done with. Didn't matter, though.

After I met Janelle for lunch that day, I was gonna take Tyler to go visit his daddy. I didn't want him to forget who he was.

An hour later, I drove in to midtown Atlanta to Taco Mac on Peachtree Street and found a spot in the parking garage. When I walked into the restaurant, I saw Janelle with Tyler sitting at a booth, waiting for me. Janelle had ordered some fries and was feeding them to Tyler.

He looked so much like his father. Janelle had him in a high chair, dressed in his little blue overalls and a mini red polo shirt. He was munching away at his fries when he looked up and spotted me.

"Mommy," he beamed.

"Hey, baby," I crooned and kissed him. "You been a good boy for Auntie Janelle?"

He smiled. "Yes."

"He's been a very good boy, Nikki," Janelle confirmed. "He loves his auntie!"

I had a seat at the table. "I can't thank you enough for taking him for the night."

Janelle looked at me oddly. "You know Jayson and I don't mind watching our godson, but this was the third time this week, Nikki. Is everything okay?"

I smiled nervously. "I'm fine. It's just with Dre gone, I've had to work some extra hours at the store."

"Really, Nikki? 'Cause last time I was there, Penny told me you were taking some time off and she was running the store. You've been kind of MIA this whole week. So what's really going on?" Janelle was no dummy. She knew me better than I knew.

The waitress walked up to the table, giving me an escape from her question. After we placed our orders, I turned my attention to Tyler.

"Nikki . . ."

"I'm going to take Tyler to see Dre this afternoon," I told her before she could ask her question again.

"That's good, but you're avoiding my question. What's going on with you?"

I sighed. "Janelle . . . I . . ." I didn't wanna lie to her, but I couldn't tell her the truth. "I can't tell you."

She pursed her lips together. "Me? You can't tell me of all people? Nikki, what the hell is going on? Nikki, if you're in trouble, I wanna help."

"I'm not in trouble. I just need to handle this by myself. Listen, Janelle, you have your own life now and you have Jayson. I was foolish enough to get you involved in the life years ago, and it was the wrong thing to do. Trust me. When the time is right, I'll let you know what's up, but for right now, just let me handle this," I begged her.

Janelle looked at me with concern. I knew she wanted to help me regardless, but Malachi was just way too dangerous for her to get mixed up with.

"Okay." She shook her head. "I'ma let you do what you need to do for now, but you're going to tell me everything soon. You're my family, and I love you, Nikki. Anything that affects you affects me."

"I know."

"Besides, you have to worry about Tyler now. He needs you more than ever."

"I'll do whatever I need to do in order to protect him, Janelle. You don't have to worry about that," I assured her.

And I'll do anything to protect Dre, too, I thought to myself.

***

After we finished up lunch, Janelle went home and I drove to Emory Hospital a few blocks away from Taco Mac with Tyler. I hated not telling Janelle what was going on with me, but it was for her own good.

I took the elevator to Dre's floor and carried Tyler in my arms to his room. When I walked in Dre's room, my heart dropped into my stomach. I nearly dropped Tyler as well. My eyes scanned the room from left to right, but it was empty. Dre was gone!

9

Marked For Death

Buckhead, GA

MALACHI

I decided to take my daughter Courtney to Lenox Mall to buy her a few things, and of course Latoya had to bring her ass along too. The only two things her ass was good for was lying on her back and spending my money. At least this little shopping spree would shut her damn mouth and keep her out of my hair. I had other concerns on my mind, like what pussyhole had the nerve to rob a shipment of cocaine from me.

They killed Jorge and his men and took my shit! Even more disturbing was that they knew where Ricky was going to meet Jorge, which told me this was an inside job. I didn't trust no man, so anybody could have been a suspect. Lucky for Ricky I knew he wasn't involved because of the eyes I had watching him in his crew. So that meant somebody else was doing this. My brother Reggie wasn't smart enough to pull that off without fucking it up, so that took him off my list. So who else was that fucking stupid?

As I was lost in thought about this situation, Latoya walked up to me in Neiman Marcus with her hand out. "Give me your card."

I glared at her. "What did you say to me?"

She rolled her eyes. "I gotta pay for these clothes."

"You mean I gotta pay for these clothes. Watch how you ask me for my card."

"Whatever," she said and rolled her neck. "Shit gotta be paid for."

"Watch you blood-clot mouth," I growled through clenched teeth. I wanted to snap her neck right there in the store.

"Or what? You gonna hit me? The mother of yo' child," she dared.

She didn't know how close to the edge she was. "You stupid bitch—"

"Oh, no you didn't just talk to me like that!"

"Keep pushing me, Toya, and you have no idea how close you are."

"You another one of them crazy-ass Jamaican men, Malachi," she quipped. "You don't want the drama I'ma bring to you if you put your hands on me."

I grabbed her by her arm and snatched her closer to me. Latoya was shocked, and fear had replaced the arrogance in her face. My grip was so strong I could have yanked her arm out of her socket.

"Ow! You're hurting me, Malachi!"

"I know. Don't think for a second you're untouchable, because you can come up missing one day," I uttered to her menacingly.

Her eyes widened like saucers and my message became clear to her.

"Mommy, I wanna go," Courtney yelled, saving her mother.

I let her go, and she pulled herself together before Courtney realized the tension between us. "Okay, baby. I was just asking your daddy for something."

I handed her my black card, and Courtney ran up to me and hugged my leg.

"Daddy, can you buy me some ice cream too?"

"Anything for my baby," I said to her and smiled. "Go with your mother to the register. I'm going to go to the restroom downstairs."

"Okay, Daddy," Courtney beamed.

"I'll meet you in the food court," I informed Latoya, and she nodded nervously.

I walked out of the store because I had to get away from that bitch before I killed her. She thought just because she was my child's mother she could play games with me. Nobody played games with Malachi Turner!

I went to the lower level of the mall into the food court and into the men's restroom. As I walked in, I noticed a nigga behind me dressed in khakis and a plaid blue button-down come in behind me. His fro was nappy, skin was a reddish tone, and he was well built. He stuck out.

I walked all the way to the end of restroom to the last urinal, and he went into a stall. I heard him pissing, so I did the same. I was on the edge, feeling paranoid. Latoya had me unfocused. I swear that bitch would be the death of me if I didn't kill her first.

I went to wash my hands and splashed some water on my face. Had to remain calm. Then I saw the red nigga again behind me in the mirror, walking up on me quick. His hands went under his shirt, and he pulled out a blade. With one swift motion, he stabbed forward.

I barely had time to move and get my guard up. The knife stabbed my left bicep. Blood sprayed the restroom mirror. He had been aiming for my neck. Pain shot through my body, but I didn't scream out loud.

Before he could pull the knife out of me, I tagged him with a nasty right to the jaw, sending him to the floor, I staggered back. He recovered quickly and was on his feet. We mean-mugged each other for a second. I yanked the blade out of my arm and threw it on the ground behind me.

"Who sent you?"

He didn't respond, but instead he pulled out a second blade and attacked me again. He slashed at my face, but I avoided his attack. I could feel my blood soaking my arm. He slashed at me again, and I grabbed his arm. My other hand grabbed his neck, and he gasped for air. I was trying to crush his windpipe. Physically I was bigger, stronger, and meaner.

I slung him into the mirror head first, shattering it. He dropped the second blade into the sink underneath him. Then I repeatedly smashed his head against the broken glass. He tried to break my grip, but it was too strong. They had sent a man to kill a beast.

"Who fucking sent you?" I yelled, smashing his head against the mirror again. A bloody smear painted the glass behind him.

He grimaced. "Fuck you!"

My hand squeezed tighter, cutting off his air supply. His face turned blue. I decided to return the favor and picked up the blade out of the sink and stabbed him in the arm. He let out an excruciating groan. Then I took the blade and entered his stomach repeatedly. I dropped him on top of the counter.

He fought for his last breaths before I slashed his throat open, letting the red crimson in his neck fill the white sink.

I had to move fast. I didn't know if there were more assassins in wait for me. I picked up both of his blades and put them in my pocket. My fingerprints were on them, and I couldn't leave them behind. I ripped my sleeve off and wrapped it around my bicep, stopping the bleeding.

Then it hit me. Courtney. She was there in the mall with killers after me. I pulled out my gun from the small of my back, underneath my shirt. I didn't need it to deal with this pussyhole, but I didn't know who else was out there for me.

I grabbed my cell and dialed Stan's number. He picked up on the first ring. He was in the car in the parking lot.

"Boss—"

"Get in here! Niggas are here to kill me," I growled to him.

"Where are you?"

"The food court! I'm coming out now! Protect my daughter," I commanded as I crept out to the restroom exit. I hung up.

I was covered in blood, holding a gun. I was going to have to move fast. A woman walking by stared at me oddly, and I mean-mugged her. She quickly moved on. I walked quickly through the food court to the exit, tucking my gun under my shirt.

I spotted Latoya and Courtney sitting at a table, waiting for me. Good. She was safe. But then I saw danger.

The red nigga hadn't been alone. I spotted four of them by the exits, looking at me. They were wearing shades and dressed in big jackets. My daughter was in the middle.

I moved to the other side of the food court through the crowd of people. The killers moved with me, away from Latoya and Courtney. Another person noticed my bloody arm and pointed me out to his friend.

I brushed by a few more people, and the assassins closed in on me. They were twenty-five, maybe thirty feet away. They weren't going to let me escape the food court, so I decided to draw first blood. I aimed my cannon and let thunder explode from the barrel. I hit a killer in the face, giving him a closed casket funeral. Blood sprayed all over people walking by.

"Bring it on, pussyholes!" I yelled.

Pandemonium erupted as the people in the food court shrieked and ran for cover. The killers pulled out their steel and returned my hollow tips. Men screamed like bitches.

Bodies hit the ground as I dove behind the counter of an Auntie Anne's. Mayhem had just been let loose as Lenox Mall had just turned into Afghanistan. Bullets couldn't tell who was an innocent bystander in this war. Pools of blood covered the floor as the gunmen took cover behind pillars and restaurant counters. Balls of fire flew over my head. They had me boxed in. I only had a few more bullets in my clip. Death was closing in on me.

"Yuh coming for me?" I defiantly shouted. "Yuh bumbaclot coming for me? Yuh want to murda me? Come get me, pussyholes! I got hot fire for yuh rasshole! I murda yuh all!"

I should have seen this coming. Then my heart dropped into my belly as I saw her.

"Daddy!" Courtney yelled as she broke free from Latoya.

A gunman turned and aimed his cannon at her, and thunder erupted.

NIKKI

Dre was gone. His room looked like it hadn't been occupied in days.

Fear washed over me, and I quickly ran out of the room with Tyler in my arms. I spotted a nurse walking by.

"Where's Andre?" I yelled frantically.

"Ma'am?"

"Andre Wade! He was in room 415!"

"Ma'am, calm down."

"Don't tell me to calm down. Tell me where my man is!"

I didn't care how loud or rude I was. I wanted answers. Tears filled my eyes, and Tyler started to cry too, seeing me so distressed.

"Okay, let me find out," the white nurse said calmly. She ran to the nurses' station.

He couldn't have died. All this time I didn't see him. I hugged Tyler tightly as tears ran down my face. I didn't know if he was trying to console me or I was trying to calm him down.

The nurse called to me. "Miss Bell?"

"Yes. Where's my fiancé?"

"Two days ago, Andre Wade was taken into protective custody by the FBI."

"The FBI? Why?"

"The FBI said because they found the same shell casings at the scene of a homicide that were used in his shooting, they decided to keep him somewhere undisclosed."

"But that's my child's father! How will I know if he's all right?"

"Ma'am, you'll have to contact the FBI."

She turned and walked away, and I was left even more confused than ever. On the one hand, I should have been glad Dre was under protection, but I had no idea where he was. I had to find out where he was, but in the meantime, I could tell Malachi to kiss my ass!

10

Relaxers

Buckhead, GA

MALACHI

A gunman turned and aimed his cannon at Courtney and thunder erupted. The sound of an AK-47 ripping through flesh and leaving brain matter all over the food court floor came next.

Bump had followed my orders to the letter and protected Courtney by murdering the gunman aiming for her. The other two assassins decided to break out and escape through the restaurant exit.

"Daddy?" Courtney looked around, confused and scared.

"Courtney!" Latoya yelled and ran to her.

I jumped over the counter and ran to her as well. She hugged me tight.

"Boss! We have to go," Bump advised.

"Yes, you did good," I told him. I looked at Latoya. She was shook. "Come!"

We ran out of the mall with Bump leading the way to the parking lot, and jumped in the back of the Bentley. Bump burned out of the mall parking lot, and in minutes we were on the Georgia 400 North, heading to a safe house. Latoya was still holding Courtney tight, neither one saying a word. My little girl had seen death for the first time. Her innocence had just been lost.

As silence enveloped the car, we all heard a knocking noise coming from the trunk.

"What is that?" Latoya asked me.

"Bump, what's in the back?"

"After you called me, I spotted a nigga in the parking lot with a gat waiting, so I crept up on him and knocked his ass out and put him in the trunk. Figure you may wanna ask him some questions," Bump informed me.

"Yes, I have a few questions indeed."

Twenty minutes later, we got to a safe house in Alpharetta. Couldn't take a chance of going home to Dunwoody. Could be more killers waiting for me. I called Ricky and Reggie and told them to meet me there and to bring the crew. This was now war, and I needed my soldiers with me.

I called my personal doctor to come clean and stitch up my wound. He was there within a half hour to bandage up my stab wound.

After I made sure Courtney and Latoya were safely settled in the house, I went down to the basement, where Bump was working on the asshole that came to murder me. I came downstairs with a plastic bag filled with things I needed, and the fool was tied to a chair as Bump pounded his face with his massive fists.

The bastard was tough. He was still mean-mugging Bump, not saying a word. I needed answers. I needed to know who was coming after me, and simply killing this nigga wasn't what I needed to happen.

"Bump."

He paused and looked at me.

"What has he said?"

"Nothing yet."

Just then Ricky and Reggie came down the stairs and joined us.

"Boss, who's this?" Ricky asked.

"One of the pussyholes who came to murda me."

"All the news channels are talking about what went down at Lenox Mall, Malachi. They calling it a blood bath," Reggie informed me.

"Any mention of me?"

"No. They don't have any video or anything posted yet. The police are still investigating it," Ricky told me.

I turned and looked at the nigga in the chair. "Who hired you?"

He didn't say anything, and Bump punched him again, but he barely grunted.

"Don't waste your energy, Bump. A nigga like this won't break like this." I stared at his bruised and battered face and noticed his bald head had lumps too. "But you will tell me what I need to know. This is your last chance to tell me what I want to know."

"Fuck you. You might as well go 'head and kill me now," he snarled.

I grinned at him. "Fine. Have it your way."

I pulled out of the bag a pair of plastic gloves and put one on my right hand. Then I reached back in the plastic bag and took out a bottle of Courtney's Dark and Lovely kid perms, and the nigga in the chair looked at me oddly.

"Malachi, what the fuck you gonna do with that?" Reggie inquired.

I didn't answer him. I took my hand with the glove on it and scooped out a handful of the white cream and then slapped it on the nigga's bald head.

"What the fuck you doing?" he yelled.

Bump grabbed him and held him still as I smeared the cream all over his head. Soon his head was covered with the creamy white relaxer.

"I'll be back in an hour, and we'll see if you feel like talking then."

"Fuck you, man!"

I smiled and peeled off the glove and tossed them on the ground. Bump, Reggie, and Ricky followed me back up the stairs.

"I don't get it. Why you did that for?" Reggie asked.

"You'll see."

An hour later, I heard an excruciating scream coming from the basement. I marched back down the stairs with Big Bump, Reggie, and Ricky, and saw that nigga on his side, still tied to the chair, trying to rub the relaxer cream off of his head with no success. The chemical burns on his head were literally peeling away the flesh on his scalp as red blisters covered his head. He was yelling and crying like a baby for relief.

"Get it off!" he shouted.

"You feel like talking yet?"

"Yes! Please! Aarrgh," he squealed.

"Give me a name."

"Don P! Don P!"

I looked at Ricky and Reggie to see if they had heard of a Don P, and both of them shook their heads. "Never heard of him."

"Please! He's called Don P! Please get it off me," he begged.

He wasn't lying, but the name Don P meant nothing to me. "Where is he from?"

"What!"

"Is he local?" I asked him.

"I don't know! He . . . argh . . . just calls us and wires money to our accounts!"

I looked at him in agony and realized he had no information worthwhile for me. He was just a hired gun sent to murder me. I still had no idea who was coming for me. This was a fucking waste of time.

"All right. I believe you." I looked at Bump. "Take care of him."

Bump pulled out his .45.

The nigga's eyes widened. "What! But I told you—"

Thunder exploded from the end of the barrel. Bump put three slugs in his chest and ended his misery.

I still had no answers but I did have a name. I turned and faced Ricky. "Find out who the fuck is Don P."

"I'm on it, boss."

JASMINE

"Breaking news. Three hours ago, gang violence erupted in Lenox Mall, killing six people. Included in the dead are three gunmen. We're also told one victim was found in the restroom, stabbed to death. Police have made no arrests in the incident. Witnesses are saying a black man opened fire in the middle of the Lenox food court, killing a man. Three other men dressed in black drew weapons and returned fire. We will bring you more updates on this breaking story as more information comes in," the news reporter on Channel 2 announced as I put on my jacket.

What the fuck was wrong with these young niggas these days? You couldn't even go to the fucking mall without catching a bullet in your ass.

I turned off the TV and grabbed my keys. I was on my way to make some money at The Pink Palace, and

I was running late. My mind was still wondering what the connection between Malachi and Nikki was and if it was going to interfere with my hustle at the club.

I got to The Pink Palace thirty minutes later, and the fucking place was half empty! Where the hell was everybody? It was Saturday night. The place should have been jumping by then.

I glanced onstage and saw a couple of chicks poppin' their shit for a few niggas, but that looked like chump change to me. I looked up to Malachi's office and nobody was there.

I headed backstage to see who was there. As I walked in the dressing room, I saw Kandi with three other bitches, sitting at her dressing table, laughing and carrying on like it was happy hour or some shit.

Hmph, I guess Kandi has finally come out of her shell and made some "friends."

She was sitting in this one chick's lap called Hester. Hester was a Filipino bitch that looked like a thicker version of that singer Cassie, without the half shaven-off hair. The other two bitches were Jade, a curvy chocolate honey with weave all the way down to her ass, and Safire, a thick-ass redbone with tittes so big that they could give shade to a small child. Kandi had no idea how scandalous these hoes were.

I cleared my throat, and Kandi turned and saw me.

"Hey, Jasmine." She got up off of Hester's lap.

Hester rolled her eyes at me but wisely didn't say shit to me. They knew I didn't play that shit. I was the queen bitch there.

Jade and Safire smirked and giggled to themselves.

"Hey, what's going on?"

"Nothing. We're just here chillin'," Kandi responded nervously.

Hester rose up out of her seat. "We'll holla at you later, Kandi."

"Okay."

Hester, Jade, and Safire walked away from us, still giggling and shit.

"What the hell is so funny?" I asked Kandi.

She shrugged her shoulders. "I don't know."

I knew it shouldn't bother me, but Kandi was kind of my protégé, and I didn't like the way those hoes were all up on her like that. I didn't like the idea of anybody taking advantage of her, other than me. Just looking at Kandi, she seemed a bit off to me for some reason.

"You better be careful around them hoes."

"Them?" She pointed in their direction. "They're harmless."

I walked over to my mirror and took off my jacket. "You think so?"

"We were just hanging out. What's so bad about them?"

"Nothing is wrong with them, until they got your ass buck naked in a *Booty Talk* DVD, eating them out."

"Like you did me," she retorted.

I turned and looked at her. Since when did she come slick to me?

Kandi caught my vibe and looked away. "I mean, we were just kicking it. Ain't anybody out there in the club anyway."

"Hmph, true."

She was definitely a little off, and now I could see why by the white dust on her dressing table. "By the way, you got a little powder on your nose."

Kandi got a stunned look on her face and wiped her nose.

"If you gonna do that shit, then I suggest you be a little more discreet about it. Them hoes will get your ass open and hooked on that shit if you ain't careful."

"Oh . . . okay," she sheepishly replied.

"When was the last time you talked to your boy-friend?" I asked her.

Kandi flopped down in the chair next to me. "A few days. Maybe a week. I thought you said I should forget that nigga."

"Yeah, but maybe I spoke too soon. Listen, Kandi, I ain't your mother, but just be careful fucking with these bitches around here."

"Okay," Kandi said halfheartedly.

Anyway, I didn't want to waste more time babysitting that girl. It was time to make some money. I got undressed and put on my pink teddy and a pair of red Steve Madden stilettos and reapplied my makeup. Once I was pleased with what I saw in the mirror, I made my way back out to the front of the club, and it was still half dead.

I walked over to the bar, and Gina the bartender made me my usual Long Island Iced Tea.

"What the fuck is going on, Gina? Where is everybody?"

"I'm not sure, Jasmine, but I keep on hearing rumors about somebody in the streets beefing with Malachi."

"Really? Who would really want it with him?"

"Don't know, but I hear there was a big hit on some Mexican drug dealers the other night, and they were supplying Malachi," she informed me.

I took a sip of my drink. "Hmmm, that's not good. Folks are probably scared to come up in here."

"Plus there was some shit that went down at Lenox Mall this afternoon that's got everybody buzzing."

"I heard about that on the news before I left," I told her.

Just then the club doors opened and Bump was leading the way, with Malachi behind him, followed by Reggie, Ricky, and ten or twelve other niggas marching up toward his office. Malachi had a mean mug on his face like I'd never seen before. Bump scanned the club and posted niggas up around The Pink Palace.

Malachi headed up to his office, and Bump, Ricky, and Reggie went with him. Damn. I'd never seen Malachi with so much security around him before, and then it dawned on me: That shootout that went down in Lenox. Was Malachi there?

11

Obsessed with me

College Park, GA

NIKKI

I'd been calling the police and FBI for hours, and nobody would give me any information about where Dre was. This was crazy! How could they move him and not tell his family where? Well, at least I could assume he was safe, but it still killed me inside that I didn't know where he was.

I sat back in my chair in the living room as Tyler watched *Marvel Superhero Squad* on Cartoon Network. The more I thought about the situation, the more I realized I had no reason to ever return to The Pink Palace. I was supposed to be there that night, but fuck that, and fuck Malachi! He couldn't hold Dre's life over my head anymore. The FBI was probably hot on his tail! Good.

It felt like it had been a long time since I'd spent the night home with Tyler. It was past his bedtime, but he was enjoying his show so much I didn't want to pull him away. Besides, I enjoyed watching him be a kid.

Those past few weeks being back at The Pink Palace had brought back so many bad memories. I couldn't believe how deluded I was into thinking that being a stripper/ho at that club was my calling in life. The stupid shit I did for money and all the lowlife pigs I fucked with to get it . . . I even dragged my poor cousin Janelle into that fucked-up lifestyle. Talk about the blind leading the blind.

I was so glad Dre had never given up on me. He loved me with my flaws and all, and we helped each other turn our lives around. We had a son. We had a new life. And now because of Malachi, he wasn't there.

A few minutes later, Tyler's show went off, and I went and picked him up. "It's time for bed, big guy."

"Okay. Where's daddy?" Tyler asked.

I stared at him, and I honestly didn't know what to say to him. "He's . . . working, baby. He'll be home soon." I wished that were the truth. "Come on, baby. Do you wanna sleep in Mommy's bed tonight?"

He nodded his head and I took him up to my room.

I spent the weekend at home with Tyler, catching up on being a mother. My thoughts were still with Dre, but I had no idea where he was, and the FBI wasn't confirming or denying putting him in protective custody. I had to figure out what was going on, but I had no idea how.

The next day, I dropped Tyler off at the babysitter's and headed to the shop. When I walked in, Penny saw me, and her jaw nearly hit the floor. It had been a while since I'd been in. She'd been running things pretty good. She was sitting behind the counter ringing a customer out.

"Nikki, I must be dreaming! I wasn't expecting to see you here today," Penny said.

"I know, right?" I walked behind the counter and gave Penny a hug. "I didn't think I would be here today either."

"So what's going on with you and Malachi?" Penny asked.

I frowned and sat on the stool next to Penny. "Forget that nigga. I got bigger concerns. Dre has been put in protective custody by the FBI, and they won't tell me where he is."

"What! How can they do that and not tell you?"

"That's what I'm trying to figure out. I've been calling them since Friday, but they won't give me any information. I'm so worried about him, Penny. I have no idea what condition he's in. Even Tyler has been asking for his daddy, and I don't know what to tell him."

Penny put her hand on my shoulder. "We'll figure this out, Nikki."

I spent the day working in the shop with Penny, catching up with some of the bills that had been piling up. I was lucky business was still steady, because our savings were dwindling.

I made a few more calls to the FBI but was still not getting any more information on Dre. I was at my wit's ends on what to do. I left the shop at 5:30 to pick Tyler up at the babysitter's and then pop into Wal-Mart on the way home to pick up a few groceries for the house.

I pulled into my driveway and got out of the car, and then I saw a limo pull up in front of my house. I knew who it was as soon as I saw it. Bump got out of the driver's side and opened the door for Malachi.

He stepped out dressed in a gray two-piece suit and black loafers. He walked over to me by my car and gave me a frown. I returned his frown with one of my own.

"What the hell do you want?" I asked.

"We had an agreement, Nikki. You haven't been at the club in three nights. You know what the consequences of breaking our arrangement would mean."

"Things changed." My mind was racing, trying to think of what I could say, and then it came to me. "You can't hold Dre's life over my head anymore. He's dead."

A surprised expression came over his face. It was a lie, but I didn't want to warn him of the FBI being involved in his relocation.

"I'm sorry to hear that, Nikki."

"Whatever. You got exactly what you wanted. My baby's father is dead! Now get the hell out of my life!"

He stared at me blankly as if what I said meant nothing to him. I turned to get Tyler out of the car, and he grabbed my arm.

"Get the fuck off me!" I yelled.

"Quiet," he said with authority. "I normally would have slapped you down for talking to me like that, but I understand you're emotional right now, so I'll excuse it."

"You're outta your damn—"

"I said be quiet! I don't give a damn about Dre, but you . . . you interest me. I've never met a woman quite like you, Nikki." He paused and let my arm go. "Regardless of Dre's untimely death, we still had an agreement. Dre's debt has been passed on to you, and I will still collect."

"Fuck you!"

He gave me a menacing glare and got in my face. "Oh, you will. You will also be at The Pink Palace this Saturday night, ready to work, or your son will be growing up in foster care. Your fine ass brings a lot of money to the club, and I don't plan on losing you."

I couldn't believe my ears! "You're fucking crazy!"

He grabbed my throat, and it felt like he was choking the shit outta me. Tyler started to cry, seeing his mother attacked.

"I warned you about your mouth, Nikki. You will respect me. Is that understood?"

I nodded my head and he let me go. I fell to my knees, trying to catch my breath. This crazy-ass nigga would have killed me right in front of my son.

"Good. So I'll see you at the club Saturday night. You're a gorgeous woman, Nikki, and if you behave yourself, you'll see what I can do for you. I did you a favor getting rid of that bum-ass nigga Dre. You'll see what a real man can do for you."

I stared up at him with disgust. If I could, I would have put a bullet between his eyes.

He gave me an evil smirk then turned and went back to his limo. Bump opened his door and then got in and drove off.

I got up off the ground and opened the car door and consoled Tyler.

"Its okay, baby. Mommy is okay," I whispered to him, wishing that were true. I was trapped, and Malachi had no intention of letting me be free. I protected Dre, but at what cost? Why was he so fucking obsessed with me?

MALACHI

I had noticed that Nikki didn't show up all weekend, so I knew something was up. I hated being so rough with Nikki, but her spirit had to be broken before she became my lady. Dre dying was only a bonus.

I'd have to send Ricky to the hospital to confirm her story, and if he wasn't dead, to put a bullet in his head. Either way, I was done dealing with him.

Nikki was the type of lady I could mold into the perfect lady for me. More than that whore Latoya could be.

Things were still uneasy with this mystery nigga Don P coming after me. I still had no idea who this nigga was. No word on the street on who this pussy-hole was or where he came from, so I had to take extra precautions and have more security around me at all times.

In the meantime, I needed to find a new supplier since Jorge had been killed. I had made contact with a Cuban named Carlos in Miami, who I know worked with some nigga up in New York called King before he got murdered. I had to move fast and reestablish my grip on the Atlanta scene before these other small-time pushers decided to move in on my turf.

The next Saturday was the annual Hot 107.9 Birthday Bash Concert, and it was going to be a big night at The Pink Palace. I needed my best dancers in the house because I had a special appearance by Kane, Beata Douglas, and the Flip Set Family scheduled to be in the club. Between Nikki and Jasmine, I was going to make a killing! And if this Don P wanted to come after me, I'd be ready for him too.

12

Just like me

Smyrna, GA

Jasmine

Going home was never an easy thing for me. I loved my parents, but because of my choices in life, things were strained, especially with my father. They knew about my lifestyle and were very disappointed with my decision.

My mother had come to terms with it, even though she disapproved. My father bareley said two words to me, but I didn't care. He liked to sit there and judge me, but he didn't want to look at the skeletons in his own closet, like the mistress he'd had for the last twelve years that my mother turned a blind eye to. She busted him having an affair with a teacher at the school where he coached football. He begged my mother to forgive him for months, until she broke down and let him back in her life. She was so weak at times. He swore that it was over, but I didn't trust any man. At least I was up front with my life and not lying to anybody about it.

The only reason I visited was because of my mother and her heart condition. She had congestive heart failure three years ago and had a triple bypass. I drove down to Smyrna every two weeks or when I could.

Despite all the things we disagreed on, I still loved my mother very much. I made sure if there was anything she needed, I bought it for her. I felt like my father resented that I had money like that to spend, but that was his problem.

I pulled up to the house and used my key to open the front door. I saw my mother sitting on the couch, watching Judge Judy.

"Hey, Mom."

"Jacqueline." My mom always called me by my full name. I almost at times forgot that was my name. "How are you, darling?" She stood up and gave me a hug.

"I'm fine, Mom. How are you?"

"Oh, I'm getting by. Every day is a gift from God."

I had a seat next to her. "So your breathing has been fine?"

"Yes, baby, only when I walk for long distances it becomes a little short, but the exercise is still good for me."

"But don't overdo it. I don't want you to end up in the hospital again," I warned her.

"Hush. I'll be fine." She paused then looked at me. "How are you, Jacqueline?"

"How do I look?" I leaned back, showing off how good I looked in my BCBG dress and Gucci pumps. "I'm doing great, Mom."

"So you're still dancing at that club?" she said in a disapproving tone.

"Yes, I am."

"Why, Jacqueline? You're so smart and so beautiful. Why do you sell yourself short? You're a college graduate. You can be doing a number of things instead of that."

I sighed and leaned back. "Like I said plenty of times, Mother, I'd rather be my own boss, making my own money. I'm not just a stripper. I'm a business. I model. I sell my calendars and posters. I'm independent. I just don't feel like I have to be a part of corporate America to live the American dream."

"So dancing naked in front of perverted men is the American dream? We didn't raise you to be like this, Jacqueline."

"No, you didn't. I choose this life. I'm happy. More happy than you are, being here with him, putting up with his nonsense," I retorted.

My mom sighed. I knew it was a low blow, and I regretted throwing it up in her face.

"Don't disrespect your father."

"But he can disrespect you?" I could see the embarrassment on her face. "I'm sorry, Mom. I didn't mean that. I just don't wanna have this argument every time I come to see you. I know you don't like my lifestyle, but I'm still your daughter, and I still love you. I just want you to accept me as I am."

She put her hand on mine. "I love you no matter what, Jacqueline. I just want you to be truly happy. Do you ever talk to Rashida and Joyce anymore?"

Rashida and Joyce were my childhood friends. I would never admit this to anybody, but I systematically destroyed those friendships because of my jealously of Rashida's relationship. I was in love with her, and when she didn't return my feelings, I purposely set out to ruin her relationship with her man. In the process, I wrecked our friendship forever. It was one of the few regrets I did have. I wished I could change that.

"No, I don't. I . . . really don't wanna talk about them, Mom."

"Okay, baby." She stared at me. "You do look beautiful, even with all that makeup on."

I chuckled. "Thanks, Mom."

I spent most of the day with her, eating lunch and talking. It felt good being with her. I felt like regular old Jacqueline Dawson again, not Jasmine the stripper. It was good to get away from it every now and then. I was enjoying spending time with her so much I forgot what time it was until I heard my dad's truck pull up in the driveway.

He came into the house and saw me sitting next to Mom. She got up and greeted him at the door.

"Hello, baby." She gave him a kiss.

He stared at me with those judging eyes,."Jacqueline."

I returned the glare. "Douglas."

Another awkward silence filled the room. He walked by and put his bag down by the couch and walked into the kitchen.

"Well, I guess that's my cue that it's time to go."

"You don't have to leave, Jacqueline. This is your home too."

I rolled my eyes. "Not anymore. I gotta get going anyway. I love you, Mom."

"I love you too, darling."

I gave her a kiss and bounced up outta there. As much as my mom would have wanted us to be father and daughter again, I knew he'd never accept me the way she did. I'd be damned if I put up a front for him. I was who I was, and I didn't make any excuses about that.

A couple of days later, it was time to get back on my grind. After I did some digging, I found out from one of Malachi's boys that the gunfight at Lenox Mall was a hit on Malachi. I guess he wasn't fazed by the attempt on his life.

That was a week ago. Today was Hot 107.9 Birthday Bash concert, so that meant it was gonna be a big night at The Pink Palace. Every celebrity in Atlanta from Jermaine Dupri to Usher might be coming through The Palace doors, not to mention the Flip Set Family performing that night was gonna bring out the niggas with green in their pockets! The Pink Palace was going to be extra thick, and I planned on being the center of attention, getting all the money.

I went to the Birthday Bash concert at Philips Arena with Kandi and got my drink on, enjoying the music, but then we left early in order to get dressed for the club. I put on my black teddy and red Steve Madden stilettos and made sure I looked flawless. Kandi put on a new white bikini I bought her and white platform shoes. She was looking like a little sex kitten.

"Damn, Jasmine, you look fabulous," Kandi crooned.

"I know. You look sexy yourself, thanks to my styling tips. So are you ready to get this money tonight?"

"Yeah, but it looks like she is too," Kandi said and pointed past me.

"Who?"

I turned and saw Nikki looking in the mirror, wearing a sheer black teddy, looking like a cross between Meagan Good and Naomi Campbell. I hadn't seen her there in a minute, and now she just popped up. I hated to admit it, but she looked good—gorgeous to be more accurate. She had body that was built like a brick house!

I walked over to her, and Kandi followed behind me.

"Wow, don't you look sexy," I crooned.

She looked at my reflection in the mirror behind her and rolled her eyes. "What do you want, Jasmine?"

"Dang, why you gotta be like that?"

She didn't reply and continued to apply her makeup.

"So where have you been?"

She turned around. "Listen, Jasmine, I'm here to work. We don't have to make small talk with each other."

"Fine. Just as long as you know who the top bitch is here." She smirked at me. "You find that shit funny?"

Nikki shook her head. "You just remind me of somebody I knew a few years ago."

I frowned. "I ain't like nobody else, baby girl."

"That's just what I used to think," she remarked and walked away.

What the hell was that supposed to mean? I followed her out to the club floor, and I saw Nikki take the main stage. The club was packed with men and women with dollar bills in their hands, and it was standing room only. It looked like everybody that was at the concert came to The Pink Palace to get loose.

Then I heard the DJ announce, "Ladies and gentlemen, The Flip Set Family is in the house!"

I looked up to the VIP area and saw Kane, Beata Douglas, Ill Tech, and their new female rapper called Mocha G. Kane looked so damn fine with his muscular arms in his black Avirex shirt and black jeans on. He had an iced-out platinum chain around his neck.

A gang of dancers and groupies flocked toward the VIP area, but security stopped them from entering. I could see why Beata Douglas was hanging on his arm like that, to keep the hoes away from him. Beata looked thicker in real life than she looked on TV. That Gucci skirt could barely cover all that ass she had. But from what I heard on the gossip sites, it was the sexy-ass Mocha G she should have been worried about with her half naked self. If she did half the nasty shit she said in her rap lyrics, then Beata had better watch out.

I turned my eye to Malachi's office, and I saw him staring into the crowd intensely through that bullet-proof window of his. There was a lot of security up in there that night in case anything jumped off. He wasn't taking any chances.

The DJ started to play Ludacris's "How Low." I turned and looked to the center stage.

Nikki began to sidestep to the beat. She turned around and bent her knees as she slowly dropped to the floor. Then the high-pitched vocals of the song came in and Nikki started gyrating her ample ass faster, and the crowd went wild. Niggas were throwing money at her left and right!

Fuck that. She wasn't gonna outshine me on my own damn stage! I walked to the back and came from behind the pink curtains on stage with Nikki. She looked at me and chuckled, and that pissed me off even more. I jumped in front of her and started shaking my ass faster than her, making the crowd chant my name.

Nikki turned around and got in my face and started to dance just as hard as me. We were straight up battling each other on stage. Then she jumped up and did a suicide split to the floor, bouncing her ass on the stage.

I wouldn't be outdone by her, so I dropped to a split and started pussy-popping right in front of her. The crowd was going crazy, and money was falling around us like confetti.

The song ended and we stared at each other. Nikki got up and scooped up some bills and walked off stage. She turned and smiled at me again.

"Just like me."

NIKKI

That damn Jasmine was a trip. I couldn't believe how much like her I was. She thought I was there to take her spot, but that was not even close to the truth.

Malachi was forcing me to be there. It was not even about the money anymore. He just wanted me. He was a sick bastard. I had to figure a way out from under his thumb.

The Pink Palace was thick that night. I hadn't seen so many people up in there even in my heyday. Birthday Bash really packed the people in. Almost every girl was dancing on the stages or doing a lap dance for a dude or a woman.

They only let a few girls up in VIP to dance for the rappers. I wondered if Jermaine Dupri was up there. He used to pop up in there on the regular back in the day.

I was the only dancer who was not out front shaking my ass for some money at the moment. I was backstage, trying to get my mind right. I needed a drink. As I was standing backstage contemplating my fucked-up predicament, security came by with The Flip Set Family behind them.

Flip Set. That name brought back memories of that nigga Damien I used to mess with years ago. His criminal organization was called The Flip Set. They came down from New York and started locking Atlanta drug trafficking down. After Damien flipped out on his boss, King, he went back to New York, and from what I heard he helped form Flip Set Records with his cousin Rob. Kane was their first act, and now here he was, right in front of me, one of the most famous rappers in the game.

Beata Douglas was right behind him. They all had microphones in their hands, preparing to take the stage for a performance.

Beata looked up at me, and it was weird. We stared at each other for a second. It wasn't a mean mug or an envious glare. It was like with one look we understood each other.

Beata stepped over to the side of the stage where I was.

"Are you okay?"

"No . . . not yet," I answered honestly.

She stared at me for a second then spoke. "Then do what you have to do in order to be."

"Thank you."

She nodded her head then walked back over to Kane and the others. Wow, my respect for her just went up tenfold. She didn't have to take time away from what she was doing to speak to me. I guess she could just sense my misery.

The DJ got on the loudspeaker. "Ladies and gentlemen, coming all the way from New York City to The Pink Palace, performing their smash hit 'Kiss' from their debut compilation album, *United We Stand*, it's the Flip Set Family!"

The music started to play a hypnotic beat, and Kane, Beata Douglas, Mocha G, and Ill Tech all took the stage. Beata started to sing a riff then started her verse.

(Beata) Do you wanna kiss me? Baby come and kiss me. Do you wanna kiss me? Baby come and kiss me.

(Kane) She got them thick lips/ them Meagan Good lips/ I love to feel them, every time we kiss/ Like a Rogue kiss/ you draining all my powers/ but I'm feeling superhuman/ 'cause I can do you for hours/ That ass I gotta tap/ hit it from the back/ Sorry you got your hair did/ 'cause I'm pulling on that/You know what you doing/ You ain't foolin'/ got me acting

*like a fool/ when we be screwin'/ but I ain't even mad/
'cause you the baddest chick/ that I've ever had.*

*(Beata) Ooh, baby, come and put them lips on me/
Baby, I love it when you kissing me/ Baby, you got
my body shaking/ It's yours for the taking/ Come and
kiss my G-spot.*

*(Mocha G) He says I'm too mushy/ but I ain't pushy/
'cause behind closed doors he loves to kiss on my
pussy/ My mocha is so tight/ he want it all night/
I got him addicted on a chocolate high (ha ha ha) I
got them juicy lips/ the ones he love to kiss/ Do your
thing, baby. Don't stop, get it, get it/ Pucker up when
you kissing on my breasts/ You know Mocha G is the
sexiest.*

*(Ill Tech) She know she got a man/ but I got plan/
Come creep with me/ and I'll be your lover man/
Nobody else exist, baby, when we kiss/ I be lickin' all
the spots that he missed/ I can do it fast/ or I can do
it slow/ I be switchin' speeds/ when I go down below/
your waist line/ It's all mine/ Make your legs shake/
sending shivers up your spine/ We can take a trip/ to
whatever beach ya wish/ but I can make ya wet/ with
one kiss.*

*(Beata) Ooh, baby, come and put them lips on me/
Baby, I love it when you kissing me/ Baby, you got
my body shaking/ It's yours for the taking/ Come and
kiss my G-spot.*

Wow, they just tore up the stage with that song! The
crowd was going wild. They were some real talen-
ted people.

As I was looking at the crowd react to their music, I saw a familiar face in the back of the club. It was Polo, sitting at a table with Malachi's ugly-ass brother Reggie and his nigga Chaz. What the hell? I knew he did business with them, but he was also hanging out with these muthafuckas too?

I walked through the crowd, ignoring a few men asking me for a private dance, until I reached the back table.

"I guess you're a regular here these days," I said sarcastically to Polo.

He looked up at me. "Nikki?"

"Damn, girl, you thick as a muthafucka," Reggie droned.

I ignored his ugly ass. Polo got up from the table and came closer to me.

"Nikki, what are you still doing working here?"

"I can ask you the same question."

Polo sighed then gestured for me to follow him to a quieter area near the restrooms, away from Reggie's ears. Polo stared at me seriously.

"I told you, Nikki, that being here is not safe. You should be home with your son."

"If I could, I would." I turned up the corners of my lips in disgust. "So you're still here doing business with the niggas that shot your best friend? What kind of shit is that?"

Polo shook his head, "Things are not what you think. Why are you back here dancing again? Is Malachi forcing you?"

"What do you think? He's making me dance here for him!"

Polo frowned and looked up toward Malachi's office. "Muthafucka," he mumbled to himself. "You have to get out of here, Nikki. It's not safe."

"Why do you keep on saying that? What's going on?"

A guy walked out of the restroom and stared at me and licked his lips. Polo pulled me closer and put his hands on my waist and whispered in my ear. "Niggas are gunning for Malachi. They just tried to kill him in Lenox Mall a week ago."

I smiled, "Well, isn't that great news? That will solve my problems," I whispered back to him. "Who's coming after him?"

"I don't know, but I don't want you to get caught in the crossfire. I don't want anything to happen to you," Polo said to me with concern. He gazed in my eyes, and I saw that he cared for me a lot more than just as a friend. His lips were inches away from mine.

"I can't have anything happen to you. I'm going to take you home."

"Polo, I can't. Malachi will kill me if I don't dance here." I looked around to make sure nobody was watching us. "I have to go."

"Nikki—"

I pulled away from him. "I have to go."

I walked away from Polo and headed back to the stage. I had no idea he felt so strongly about me. I guess being Dre's best friend, he couldn't express himself like that. But what if I never saw Dre again? Should I have told him about the FBI? No, 'cause I didn't know why he was still doing business with Malachi's crew. I didn't know if I could trust him. But if what he said was true about niggas gunning for Malachi, then I hoped they killed his ass.

13

Revelations

Atlanta, GA

Jasmine

I ended up making a little over $6,000 at Birthday Bash night at The Pink Palace. Not bad for one night of work. The only down side was Nikki. I probably would have made more money if her ass wasn't there getting so much attention on the main stage. I couldn't believe I let her get under my skin, but the weird thing about it was that she acted like she really didn't want to be there. So what did Malachi have on her?

I knew curiosity killed the cat, but I couldn't help but wonder. Malachi called me up to his office, so he probably wanted some ass, and as long as he hit me off for my service, that was cool with me.

Security at The Palace was still deeper than a mutha-fucka as I went up the stairs to his office. Bump opened the door for me, and I saw Malachi on the phone, screaming at his workers.

"I don't want fucking excuses! Just find out who this Don P is," he growled. Then he ended the call and tossed his cell on his desk.

"Are you okay, baby?"

He looked at me and then grinned. "Don't you worry about it, sweet Jasmine. I have other concerns for you."

I raised my eyebrow. "Other concerns? Like what?"

"My dumb-ass brother Reggie's birthday is this Sunday night, and I need you and some of the girls to put on a show for him." I frowned. He smiled and continued. "Just show him a good time, and I'll make sure you'll be well compensated for your services. This is going to be a closed-door event, so ask a couple of other girls to join you."

"As much as I like to make you feel good, daddy, I'm gonna have to decline the offer. I really don't like him."

Malachi chuckled. "I told him you would say no. Are you sure you don't wanna make some extra cash?"

"I'll pass, but I'm sure Hester or Jade will jump on it."

"As you wish."

I walked around his desk and sat in his lap. "Now, is there any extra services I can do for you?" I purred in his ear as I felt his hard dick press on my ass.

"Always," he droned as he unzipped his slacks and pulled out his one-eyed monster. I slid down to my knees and gave him a deep oral massage.

After I was done servicing Malachi, I went back downstairs and saw Nikki coming in to work. Maybe I'd been going about it all wrong. I assumed Malachi had brought her in there to take my place, but I may have jumped the gun a bit.

She walked back to the locker room and started to get undressed, and I followed her. She peeped my reflection in the mirror behind her and shook her head.

"Hey, Nikki." She simply gave me a head nod. "Listen. I know we haven't gotten off on the right foot."

"We don't have to get off on any foot, Jasmine. I'm here to work, not make friends. But can I ask you a question?"

She sighed. "What?"

"Why are you here?"

She turned and looked at me but didn't respond.

"Okay, here's a better question: What does Malachi have over your head?"

"Why do you wanna know so bad?"

"I'm just curious."

"Listen, Jasmine, don't worry about me. If I were you, I would try and put as much distance between yourself and Malachi as possible. Whoever is gunning from him isn't gonna care who's standing next to him," Nikki warned.

"You mean his beef with Don P? What do you know about it?"

"Nothing much, and the less is the better. I gotta get dressed, Jasmine," she said and turned and continued to get undressed.

I walked over to my dressing table and sat down. Whoever this Don P was seemed to have Malachi taking extra precautions. Why did it feel like Nikki was more involved in all of this than she was letting on?

NIKKI

I didn't know why Jasmine was trying so hard to find out my business with Malachi, but she needed to stay out of it. I didn't trust her or anybody there in the club. For all I knew, Malachi could have been telling her to keep an eye on me in there. For that reason alone, I had a razor blade on me at all times, hidden on me just in case a bitch got rowdy. But she did confirm what Polo had told me the other night, that somebody called Don P was coming after Malachi. If he put a bullet in Malachi's head, I would be happy as hell.

What else had been playing on my mind was Polo. It seemed like he wanted to protect me more than anything else. He had almost kissed me. I never knew he felt that way for me, but with Dre somewhere out there in FBI protection, I couldn't even consider doing anything with him.

Just as I was getting ready to go out front and dance on stage, Bump stepped to me. This nigga looked like a linebacker for the Falcons with his huge self.

"Malachi wants to see you in his office."

I frowned. "For what?"

"I don't know. C'mon," he ordered.

I had no choice, so I followed him up the stairs to Malachi's office. He opened the door, and I walked in. There he was, sitting behind his big desk, smoking a cigar. I hoped he didn't think I was going to give him some ass. I had something for him if he thought that was going down again.

He exhaled a cloud of gray smoke from his mouth and grinned at me. Then he placed his cigar in his marble ashtray. "Come have a seat, Nikki."

I did as he said and sat in the chair. Malachi sat back in his black Ralph Lauren suit and continued to puff on his cigar. "I need you to come to a private party Sunday night for my little brother."

"Private party? I don't fuck for cash, Malachi," I said firmly.

"No one is asking you to. I just need you to be here at The Palace Sunday night and entertain Reggie."

"And if I don't want to?"

Malachi glared at me. "It's not a request."

"Fine." I got up and turned toward the door.

"Sit. I didn't dismiss you," Malachi said coldly.

I wanted to run, but I knew I wouldn't get far. I sat back down.

He stood up and walked around his desk and stood behind me. "I sent Ricky to check out your story about Dre being dead."

My heart sped up in my chest. Did he know that Dre was in FBI protection?

"It turns out you were telling me the truth."

"I have no reason to lie."

"Not anymore," he retorted. He placed his hands on my shoulders and caressed me. "I can't help but think about our wonderful night together. You were magnificent."

I felt so disgusted thinking about him being all over me that night. "If you say so."

"I do. You could be more than just a dancer in my club if you behave. I can make you a queen, Nikki. You need to forget about your past, because I am your future."

I pulled away from his touch and stood up. "Can I leave now?"

Malachi grinned, then with one swift motion, grabbed me by my arm and pulled me close to him. His other hand slapped and grabbed my ass roughly. I could feel his warm breath on my neck as he whispered in my ear, "I love your spirit, Nikki, and you may not believe it now, but you will be mines." He kissed my neck. "And yes, you can leave now."

He let me go, and I backed away from him. I would have spit in his face if I thought I could get away with it. Instead, I hastily walked past him and out the door and down the stairs.

If that stupid muthafucka really thought I was going to be his lady, then he must have been getting high off his own supply! Ugly-ass muthafucka! Now he had me going to some birthday/fuck party for his stupid brother Reggie. Malachi was running my life like it was his to control, and there was nothing I could do to stop it. I needed to find a way out of there and out of Malachi's life.

Perhaps I hadn't really explored all my options? Polo. I knew he was still being supplied by Malachi, but he didn't have any love for him either. Maybe there was something he could do.

After I get off of working at The Pink Palace, I made a phone call to Polo. He picked up on the second ring.

"Who this?" he answered.

"It's me."

"Nikki, are you okay?"

"Yeah. I need to see you."

"Okay. I'm over in Camp Creek right now."

"I can meet you at Chili's in ten minutes?"

"Cool. I'll see you then."

"Okay," I replied and ended the call.

I exited off of I-20 onto 285 South and head toward Camp Creek on Exit 2.

I'd known Polo for as long as I'd known Dre. His real name was Teddy, but he got the nickname Polo because he always wore polo shirts. He'd been Dre's best friend since high school, and whatever Dre decided to do, Polo was always right there by his side. The only thing Polo didn't do was get out of the drug game when Dre did three years ago. Dre encouraged him to do so but understood that Polo was a grown man, and the game and fast money could be addictive. It must've been during that time that Polo started getting his supply directly from Malachi.

I pulled into the Camp Creek Marketplace and into the parking lot of Chili's and parked. I got out and went inside, and the hostess greeted me. I then spotted Polo at a booth near the bar and made my way over to him and had a seat.

"Hey, Nikki, you look good."

"Thanks."

"I ordered some wings for us already. What you drinking?"

"A blue Margarita would be nice," I replied.

Once the waitress came over with the wings, Polo placed my drink order. I started to munch on the hot wings. I hadn't realized how hungry I was until I was on my fifth wing.

"I'm sorry, Polo. I'm just eating all your wings."

He smiled. "Don't worry about it."

The waitress came with my drink and another beer for Polo.

"I heard about Dre passing away." Polo paused then looked me in the eyes. "I'm so sorry, Nikki."

I wished I could tell him the truth, but the less he knew about Dre's whereabouts with the FBI, the better off he'd be. "It's not your fault, Polo. Malachi is to blame for all of this."

"So what's going on, Nikki? After our talk the other night, I didn't think you wanted to see me again."

I took a sip of my drink. "Polo, I don't know who's watching me in the club. I didn't want you to get in trouble being seen with me. Besides, I don't know who I can trust."

"Don't worry about me. You sounded kinda distressed over the phone. Is Malachi making you—"

"No . . . not yet." I cut him off.

Polo frowned. "I don't want you going back there, Nikki. I can take you out of town until things get settled with Malachi."

I couldn't leave town yet without knowing where Dre was. "No, I . . . I got too much invested here in Atlanta: friends, family, a business, and Tyler. Besides, Malachi would only try and track me down, or worse, go after my family here in Atlanta." I took another gulp of my Margarita. "What do you know about the niggas coming after Malachi?"

Polo took a sip of his beer. "I know they got that nigga Malachi scared shitless. It's just a matter of time before they get his ass." Polo said that with a smile on his face.

"I heard that it's somebody called Don P coming after him. Have you ever heard of him?"

"Naw, never heard of him," he said with a smile.

I stared at Polo and then it dawned on me and I put my drink down on the table. "Polo . . . are you Don P?" Polo took another sip of his beer. "Oh my God . . . Polo. Why didn't you tell me you were going to do this?"

Polo leaned in closer. "Keep your voice down, Nikki." He looked around and focused back on me, "I was going to tell you, but you kinda went off the grid. That nigga Malachi was supposed to be already dead by now, but after shit went wrong in Lenox Mall, he was rolling with almost an army around him."

I was shook. I didn't know Polo was plotting this hostile takeover this whole time. "You were behind that hit at Lenox? My God, Polo. A lot of innocent people got hurt."

"It wasn't supposed to go down like that. The niggas I got to do the job got sloppy, and that nigga Malachi is no fool." He took a sip of his beer. "Once he took out the first nigga, he was ready for war and was shooting first and asking questions later. Four of the six niggas I sent in didn't make it back."

I finished off my Margarita. "So that's why you've been hanging out at the Pink Palace so much?"

"Yeah, I been getting close to his idiot brother Reggie, finding out what Malachi's been doing for months now," Polo explained.

I looked at him with amazement. "For months! You've been planning this for months? Did Dre know about this?"

"No. Dre would never let me do this, so I had to put this in motion without him. I just never thought Malachi would put a hit on Dre before I could take his ass out."

I felt so bad now. "So that day at the hospital when I called you a coward for not going after Malachi, you were already planning to do just that. I'm so sorry, Polo."

"Don't worry about it, Nikki. I wanted to tell you so bad, but I didn't want to put you in danger. But then you started dancing in the club, and that's the last thing I wanted to see. How did that happen?"

I leaned back in my seat. "At the time, Dre was laid up in the hospital and Malachi was sending niggas to check up on his condition. I was afraid he was going to send somebody to finish the job on Dre, so I volunteered to do whatever to spare his life, and now he's dead and Malachi is holding his debt over my head."

Polo took my hand. "Don't worry, Nikki. I'm gonna make sure that nigga is dead if it's the last thing I do."

I looked in his eyes and I knew he meant every word.

"Nikki, I know you're still hurting from Dre's death, but I'm always going to be here to take care of you. I need to tell you this."

Now I felt so guilty for not telling Polo the truth about Dre being alive. "Polo . . ."

"I know, Nikki, but just hear me out. You were my best friend's lady, and I know I'm wrong for feeling like this, but I can't help it. I've been in love with you for years, Nikki."

"Oh God, Polo, you don't love me."

"But I do. I just couldn't say it because you were Dre's lady, so I didn't want to betray him like that. I'm not expecting you to say you feel the same way about me right now, but in the next few weeks, things are going to change. That nigga Malachi is gonna be dead, and I'm going to be the man running these streets."

"Polo . . . I don't know what to say."

He placed his finger on my lips and stood up. "You don't have to say a word. In the days to come, you'll see that everything I'm doing now, I'm doing it for us."

Polo kissed me then he pulled away and took a fifty-dollar bill out of his pocket and put it on the table. "Just keep on making Malachi think you're there for him, and give me whatever information you can on his whereabouts. It'll make it easy for me to finish him off."

I stared at Polo, still in shock. "Okay."

"I'll be in touch, Nikki."

He walked away, and I felt so guilty, like I was leading him on. I couldn't tell him Dre was still alive, not after he had said all that to me. Polo had orchestrated this whole takeover of Malachi and was my only way to deal with him for good. I couldn't say anything to him yet because he had to stay focused and finish the job on Malachi. But what was I going to do after that?

14

Private Party

Atlanta, GA

NIKKI

The last two days had been a blur since Polo revealed to me everything he'd been doing and how he felt for me. I never knew he'd been carrying a torch for all those years. I didn't know what was more shocking: the fact that he was in love with me, or that he was Don P, gunning for Malachi. I never would have suspected that he'd been masterminding that whole takeover by himself. I mean, Polo was not stupid, but running game on this level, I never would have thought. I had to keep the fact that Dre was still alive a secret until this was over.

It was Sunday night, and Malachi was throwing a private party for his ugly little brother Reggie. Now, back in my day, I'd fucked with niggas a lot more unattractive than Reggie, but there was something about this little foul nigga I just didn't like. Maybe it was the way he was always harassing the other dancers, the lustful looks he gave me, or maybe because he was Malachi's brother, but he really turned me off.

The Pink Palace was closed to the general public by six o'clock, and by eight o'clock, a bunch of Reggie's friends and street niggas came in. Malachi wasn't there, and that was a relief. I didn't have to look at his ass. A few other girls were already giving niggas dances, and I spotted a couple of girls getting fucked in the private VIP rooms. Back in the day, that would have been me tricking up in that room for the right amount of cash, but them days were long gone for me.

I was hoping to see Polo there that night, but I guessed he didn't make the guest list. Reggie was dressed in black jeans and a long-sleeve T-shirt with three platinum chains around his neck, acting like he was a don or some shit. With Malachi gone, I guessed he thought he was heir to the throne.

Reggie jumped up with a bottle of Nuvo in his hands. "Listen here, niggas! All these bitches here tonight are here for your entertainment, but I get the first lap dance from all of them hoes!"

Straight retard. This idiot and his boys got pissy drunk for the next couple of hours. I spent most of my time hanging with Gina at the bar, avoiding the horny niggas trying to rub on my ass.

I looked and saw Kandi, Jasmine's homegirl, with Hester and Jade, sitting at a table with some of Reggie's niggas, Chaz and them, snorting cocaine. Damn, I could tell she was being sucked into the lifestyle, and she was not going to last long at that rate.

When I had first brought Mo'Nique into The Pink Palace back in the day, I kept her clear of shit like that. Jasmine was not even there or I knew she would have objected to Kandi doing that. I would have said something, but it was not my place. I was just there to do a job, so that was what I was going to do and get the hell up outta there!

Reggie took to the stage and sat on a chair facing the main curtain. The DJ started to play Ying Yang Twins,

"The Whisper Song," and I strutted out from behind the curtain dressed in a black two-piece thong and bra set and black Gucci pumps.

Reggie's eyes bugged outta his head when he saw my thickness. I seductively moved my body, matching the rhythm of the song. Then I grabbed the pole and swung around and landed like a black panther on the prowl. I crawled my way over to Reggie in the chair and climbed up on him.

"Oh, shit," Reggie uttered to me softly and felt on my titties.

I turned around and sat on his lap and grinded my ass in his crotch, making his manhood stand to attention. I bent over and placed my hands on the stage floor in front of me and put my fat ass in Reggie's face, making my ass cheeks talk to him.

The men in the club all shouted and made catcalls at me. I rolled away from Reggie as the song ended, and I danced my way back across the stage and disappeared behind the curtain. Like always, I left them wanting more.

I headed to the empty locker room to change and get the fuck up outta there. I took off my bra and dropped it in my bag. When I looked up, I saw that ugly nigga Reggie behind me.

"What the fuck you doing in here, nigga?"

He grinned and looked at my titties and grabbed one. "I'm here to finish our dance."

I slapped his hand away. "Get the fuck off me, nigga! I ain't one of these easy hoes you fuck with!"

I guessed he didn't like that, because he rushed me, grabbing me by the neck and hemming me up on my dressing table. "Bitch, you gonna give me this pussy! It's my fucking birthday, so I get it my way!"

He was already positioned between my legs, and he reached down and ripped my thong off, exposing my pussy. Then he struggled to get his dick out of his pants.

I'd been raped before, and it was the most demeaning and disgusting thing ever done to me. Memories of the beating and raping I endured flashed back to me like it was yesterday. It had taken me a long time to get over that whole ordeal. I promised myself I would never let a nigga violate me like that again.

Unlucky for Reggie, I was able to get my hands on my razor blade I had on my dresser top. Suddenly he froze as he felt a sharp prick on his neck.

"What the—"

"Shut the fuck up!" I yelled. I had half a thought to slit his throat from ear to ear. He was lucky he was Malachi's brother, or he'd be bleeding on the ground. "Get your fucking hands off me!"

He quickly raised his hands as if he was surrendering. "Whoa, listen, Nikki. Don't—"

"I said shut the fuck up!" I roared and pressed the blade harder against his skin.

"Aaaahhhh . . . okay, okay," he yelped.

A stream of blood ran down his neck. His eyes became wide as saucers as he looked at me with fear in his eyes. I pushed him back off me.

"If you ever put your fucking hands on me again, I will kill you. Understand?"

"Yeah, okay!"

"Get the fuck out." I mushed him in the head, and he staggered back and grabbed his neck. I held the razor in my hand, ready to slice him open if he tried me again, but this little bitch didn't want none. He slowly backed away from me and left the locker room. That little creature didn't know how close he had been to losing his life on his birthday.

I waited a minute before I put the blade down and quickly got dressed into my street clothes and exited the club through the back. As I was walking to my car, I saw three niggas walking with Kandi to a car and putting her in the back seat. She looked completely fucked up, high as a bird. She could barely keep her eyes open.

I knew this was not a good look, so I rushed over to them.

"Hey! Where do you think you're taking her?" I yelled at them.

One of the niggas called Chaz, who was part of Reggie's crew, mean-mugged me.

"What the fuck does it matter to you?"

"Let her out of the car now!"

"Get the fuck outta here, bitch," Chaz barked at me.

"C'mon, man. Let's get outta here," another nigga yelled at Chaz.

"Kandi! Kandi, get out of the car," I yelled at her, but she could barely look at me. She laughed and leaned her head against the nigga next to her in the back seat.

Chaz started the engine and mashed down on the gas. I jumped out of the way at the last second before he ran me over.

I rushed back inside of the club and went over to Gina, the bartender.

"Gina, do you have Jasmine's phone number?"

"Yeah, what's up?"

"I need to her call now!"

JASMINE

The melodic sounds of Monica's "Everything to Me" resonated from my cell, waking me up from my sleep. I looked at the display and saw a 404 number I didn't recognize, so I ignored it and rested my head back on my pillow. One minute later, the phone rang again, and it was the same number. I didn't like answering numbers I didn't know, but this fucker kept on calling. I'd never get any sleep.

I pushed ACCEPT. "Who is this?"

"Jasmine, it's Nikki."

I sat up in bed. "Nikki? How did you get my number?"

"Gina gave it to me. Listen, your girl Kandi is in trouble."

"What are you talking about? What trouble?"

"She was here at Reggie's party getting fucked up."

My eyebrows crinkled. "Reggie's party? I told her not to go."

"Listen to me, Jasmine. Kandi left here with Chaz and two other niggas, and she is high as hell!"

"Oh, shit."

"You need to get here, 'cause them niggas looked like they was gonna run a train on her ass."

"Oh my God. I'll be there in fifteen minutes."

"Okay."

I ended the call and jumped up out of bed and threw on some pink Baby Phat sweats and pulled my hair back in a ponytail. One minute later, I was in my car heading toward The Pink Palace. I couldn't believe Kandi went to that damn party after I told her ass not to fuck with them!

I didn't know why I even cared so much about what happened to Kandi, but a part of me felt responsible for her. She was so damn naïve.

I raced down Peachtree Road toward the club and finally pulled into the parking lot. I saw Nikki and Gina waiting for me. I jumped out of my Mercedes-Benz.

"What the hell is going on?"

"Like I said, Jasmine, your girl Kandi got in a car with Chaz and two other niggas and took off. She was totally fucked up," Nikki explained to me.

"Who was she here with?"

"She was getting high with Hester and Jade all night," Gina informed me.

I cut my eyes to the club entrance. "Them bitches!"

I stormed toward the club, and Nikki and Gina were right behind me. When I went in, I looked around and saw niggas still partying. Reggie was in a booth, holding a napkin to his neck for some reason. Then I spotted them two scandalous hoes, Hester and Jade, giving lap dances to some niggas.

I marched over to that Filipino bitch, Hester. "You stupid bitch! Why did you let her go with Chaz and 'em?"

Hester flipped back her long, black hair and looked me up and down. "What the fuck you talking about, bitch?"

"Kandi! You dumb bitches got her high and then let that grimy-ass nigga Chaz take her outta here," I roared. My loud voice began to draw a few stares from the people around us, but I didn't give a damn.

Reggie and a couple of his niggas started to walk over to us, but then I saw Nikki mean-mugging him. She took her finger and made a cut-throat gesture across her neck. Reggie got an anxious look on his face and motioned for his niggas to go sit back down.

"I ain't her momma. She a grown-ass woman. If she wanna go make some paper, then that's her business," Hester retorted.

"But you knew she was fucked up and you still let her go. Why weren't you looking out for her?"

"Bitch, ain't that yo' job? What? You afraid Chaz is gonna stretch out that little tight pussy of Kandi's? I know you like that coochie nice and tight, Jasmine," Hester said in a sarcastic tone then licked her tongue between two fingers.

Both Hester and Jade started laughing. I snapped and grabbed Hester by her long hair. I pulled her up out of the lap of the dude she was dancing with and pulled her head back.

"Owwww," Hester yelled.

"You listen to me, bitch. If anything happens to Kandi, I'ma come back and whoop your ass!"

I gave her hair another tug, pulling her head back further. She always bragged about having real hair on her head. Guess the bitch wasn't lying, 'cause I was about to rip her shit off her scalp!

I pushed her ass forward, back into the lap of the dude she was dancing with, and she grabbed her head. Then I stepped to Jade, still sitting in the other dude's lap, and I pimp-slapped her ass across the face. I was so pissed, I wished she would try to fight back so I could break my foot off in her ass. But none of them wanted some.

I turned and walked away. Nikki was right behind me.

"Where are you going?" she asked.

"I know Chaz hustles out in Bankhead, so that's where I'm going."

We both exited out the back of The Pink Palace and walked over to my car. Nikki walked around to the passenger side.

"What are you doing?"

Nikki looked at me. "I'm coming with you."

"You don't have to do that."

"I know, but I wanna see this through to the end," she said sincerely.

I nodded my head, and we both got in my car. I pulled out of the parking lot and headed to Bankhead.

What the hell was Kandi thinking? I wanted to blame her, but I saw what she was doing with Hester and Jade, and I hadn't tried harder to stop her.

Hester had called her a grown-ass woman, but Kandi was far from grown. In all actuality, she was still very much a little girl. I should've encouraged her to work things out with her boyfriend and get the hell out of that lifestyle, but instead I decided to be her "guru" and pulled her in deeper. I even seduced her for the hell of it. Now that I thought about it, I didn't even know her real name. What the hell was I thinking?

"This is not your fault, you know," Nikki mentioned to me as we drove on the highway. "I know you think it is, but it's not."

"It is. I should have seen this coming."

Nikki looked at me. "How could you?"

I didn't have an answer.

"I've been where you are right now," she said.

"You don't have to say that to make me feel better."

"I'm not. A few years ago, I got my little cousin caught up dancing at The Pink Palace. I schooled her on the do's and don'ts of the game, and because of me, she got caught up in some real life and death shit. I should have never brought her into this game. I was lucky she got out of this lifestyle before it ruined her," Nikki confessed.

I glanced over to her. "Why did you get out? You could be running this shit by now."

She chuckled. "That's what I thought, but we both know in reality, as long as you're the one swinging on the pole, you're never gonna run this shit."

We rode in silence for a few minutes, and her words really resonated with me. I guessed she really was me a few years ago. So where did I go from there?

"What kind of car was Chaz driving?"

"A gray Dodge Charger. Have you tried calling her?" she asked.

"No. Shit. I should've been tried that." I took out my cell and speed-dialed Kandi's number. After six rings, her voice mail came on. "She's not picking up."

We soon exited off I-20 and drove down Lee Street. I really didn't fuck with this side of town if I didn't have to. Nikki seemed to know this area like the back of her hand as she navigated me through the hood like a ghetto tour guide.

This was the area that Chaz hustled at, and we drove to a few motels and didn't see his car. An hour or so passed, and still no luck. The more time that passed, the more my concern for Kandi's safety grew. We really didn't know where Chaz could have taken her.

"We're wasting our time. There's no telling where they could be," I said to Nikki.

"We have to do something. What do you know about this nigga Chaz?"

"I know he's an asshole. He runs the streets with Reggie, and he's almost as perverted as him. He's just another one of these young wannabe thugs who thinks he's the man."

"Typical," Nikki quipped.

"I just don't want anything to happen to her." My cell started to sing Monica's "Everything to Me." I looked at the display, and Kandi's name illuminated. I quickly answered.

"Kandi! Where are you?"

"Jasmine, please come . . . get me."

I pulled my car into the parking lot of a Texaco gas station/Hood Mart and parked. "Are you okay?" I asked her frantically.

"Please . . . just come and get . . . me," she responded weakly.

"Okay, baby. I just need to know where you are," I said as calmly as I could.

"I don't know."

Nikki touched my arm,

"What did she say?"

"She doesn't know where she is," I told Nikki. "Kandi, I need you to look outside and tell me what you see."

"Okay." I heard her struggling to move around, and I thought she fell off the bed. "Kandi!"

She didn't respond, but I heard her still moving. "The . . . Super 8," she mumbles.

I turned and looked at Nikki. "Where the hell is the Super 8?"

"College Park, off of Old National. C'mon, let's get back on 285 South."

I pulled out of the Texaco and headed to the highway. I tried to keep talking to Kandi, but after a second or two, she was not responding anymore, and my heart sank into my gut. I prayed that she was still alive.

Within a few minutes, we were exiting onto Old National Highway and we pulled up to The Super 8.

After we described to the night manager who we were looking for, she said she remembered her and took us to the second floor and opened room 214. When the door opened, I couldn't stop the tears from flowing down my face. Kandi was lying on the floor, buck-naked, looking like a broken doll with blood between her legs. The odor in the room was a pungent funk of pussy and dick. The mattress had blood all over it.

I rushed to Kandi's side, and by the grace of God, she was still breathing. Nikki got on her cell and called 911.

15

Preexisting Condition

East Point, GA

NIKKI

What a hell of a night. If you had told me I would be sitting there in a cold-ass waiting room in South Fulton Hospital with Jasmine, I would have laughed at you.

This whole situation hit so close to home for me. It was a little over three years earlier that I was raped and beaten like a dog by a nigga named Damien. Seeing Kandi in that condition in that hotel room, sprawled out on the floor, naked with blood between her legs, gave me flashbacks that sent chills up my spine.

Jasmine was in tears and in shock seeing Kandi like that, no doubt blaming herself for what happened. She rode in the ambulance with Kandi, while I followed behind them in Jasmine's Benz.

In the short time I'd known Jasmine, I'd never seen her like this. She reminded me so much of myself a few years ago: a money-hungry bitch using her body to get what she wanted. That reflection of myself was scary to look at now, but I guessed seeing Kandi like that broke down all of Jasmine's defenses and Ho-ology mindframe.

We were lucky Kandi carried her I.D. and, surprisingly, a Humana insurance card in her pocketbook. Her real name was Candice Ford, nineteen years old.

"She's going to be okay, Jasmine."

Jasmine looked at me sitting next to her in the chair. "Thank you for calling and telling me what happened to her. I . . . I haven't exactly been the nicest person to you."

I chuckled. "It comes with the job description: show no love to the competition in the club."

She laughed too. "Who said you were competition for me?"

"See, you're already feeling better."

She looked to the floor. "I should have done better by her. I should have kept a closer eye on her. Made sure she didn't get caught up with them nasty bitches up in there."

"You could've done all that, and this still could have happened. She made a bad decision. But she's lucky to have a friend like you," I consoled her.

"A friend like me." Jasmine shook her head. "That's a joke. I could've been a lot better."

"Then be that now."

She smiled at me. "I can do that."

We sat in silence for a few minutes. We didn't notice it at first, because we were so concerned with Kandi's condition, but we were gaining a few stares from some men in the emergency waiting room. All kinds of weirdos were up in there at that time of night.

Jasmine was wearing a tight, form-fitting pink Baby Phat sweat suit that hugged her voluptuous body, and I doubted that she had any panties on underneath. I did wake her up out of her sleep. I had just left The Pink Palace and was dressed in my True Religion jeans and a tight black Hello Kitty T-shirt that snuggled my breasts.

A dude got up from his chair and walked over to us. He just stopped and stared at us like we were a pair of steaks on the grill.

Jasmine looked at me and then we both looked at him. "What the hell are you staring at?"

"Yeah, put your fucking tongue back in your mouth and keep it moving," Jasmine snapped.

The dude got an embarrassed expression on his face and went and sat back down.

"Niggas." Jasmine shook her head. "Even when they're hurt, they dicks still control their brains."

"Typical. We're not even on the clock," I quipped.

"Speaking of which, what's up with you and Reggie?" Jasmine inquired.

"That asshole."

"Yeah, that asshole. I saw the gesture you gave him. What was up with that?"

"That little nigga thought just because I gave him a dance for his birthday that he was gonna get some ass too."

Jasmine frowned. "I hate that little ugly muthafucka. I always gotta stop him from harassing the new girls."

"Well, that nigga came back into the locker room while I'm changing and tries to take some pussy. So I grabbed my razor blade and put it to his neck! He's lucky his ass is Malachi's brother, or he would be dead right now," I told her.

"You should've slit his throat! I swear when I catch up to Chaz and them, I'm going to castrate them fuckers," Jasmine said with vengeance.

"I'm with you on that. Niggas like that need to be dealt with severely."

Just then, a male nurse dressed in blue scrubs with a chart in his hand walked out to us. He was a handsome, light-skinned brother who looked a lot like Lenny Kravitz.

"Are you friends of Miss Ford?"

Jasmine stood up. "Yes, I'm her sister. Is she okay?" Jasmine lied so she could find out what was going on with her.

"Yeah, she's doing a little better now, but she was not in good shape when she came in. We had to pump her stomach. I'm Chauncey Williams. I'm the nurse covering her room tonight."

"She was raped."

"Raped?" Chauncey looked at me oddly. "We checked her out and we didn't find any vaginal tearing. We found traces of semen, but it doesn't appear to be forced sex."

"But why was there was so much blood?" Jasmine questioned.

"Ah . . . Miss Ford started her menstrual cycle."

"Oh," I said, relieved. Chaz and the others must have bugged out when they saw her bleeding like that and left her there.

"Miss Ford had a lot of drugs in her system: cocaine, ecstasy, and alcohol. Someone with her condition should *really* not be doing these things," Nurse Chauncey stressed.

Jasmine looked at him oddly. "With her condition?"

"Yeah. Miss Ford has an enlarged heart. Her heart rate was unusually slow, so we ran some tests on her and discovered the defect."

Jasmine exhaled deeply and shook her head. "Is she going to be okay?"

"Yes, luckily—if you can call this happening lucky— you two brought her in and we can start treating her now. If she never came in, she could have had a heart attack at almost any time," Nurse Chauncey explained. "Do you wanna see her?"

"Yes, thank you."

Jasmine and I followed Chauncey back through the double doors to one of the rooms. We saw Kandi lying in bed with all kinds of tubes going up her nose, arm, and chest, running to machines beeping and monitoring her condition. Her face was puffy as she lay under a thin sheet.

"I'll give y'all some time," Chauncey said as he closed the door behind him.

Kandi opened her eyes and saw us standing next to her bed.

"Hey, Kandi, you feel better?" Jasmine asked.

Kandi nodded her head. "Yeah . . . I fucked up, huh?"

Jasmine took her hand. "Don't worry about that. Just concentrate on feeling better."

"Hey, Kandi," I said and touched her leg.

"Hey, Nikki. I'm sorry . . . I didn't listen to you."

"You weren't thinking straight. Did Chaz and them hurt you?" I asked, trying to make sure.

"I . . . don't really remember too much of what happened, but . . . I think I came on my period and grossed them out," Kandi explained.

"Don't worry about them. So how come you never told me about—"

"My heart?" Kandi finished Jasmine's sentence.

"Yeah. You should've told me."

Kandi shrugged her shoulders. "Didn't think you wanna hear about that."

Jasmine took her hand. "I do now."

JASMINE

Both Nikki and I sat with Kandi until she dozed off to sleep hours later. The poor girl was really messed up.

I decided to give Nikki a ride back to The Pink Palace to pick up her car. I was so glad she was there with me, because I was so fucked up in my heart when we found Kandi in that hotel room. I didn't think it would hit me that hard.

"Thank you for staying with me at hospital, Nikki," I said to her as I drove down the street.

"It wasn't a problem."

"Listen, whatever Malachi is holding over your head, find a way to get out of it, because once he's got a grip on you, he won't let go."

I pulled into the parking lot of The Pink Palace next to Nikki's black Cutlass Deville.

Nikki looked at me. "I know. I'm working on something. What are you going to do about Kandi?"

"I'm going to help her. She needs somebody. She needs a friend."

"Good. I guess I'll see you Wednesday night?" Nikki asked.

"Yeah, I'll see you then."

Nikki opened the car door.

"Wait."

Nikki stopped and looked at me.

"Do you still have my number in your phone?"

"Yeah."

"Well, if you need any help dealing with . . . anything, call me."

Nikki nodded and got out of my car and into hers. After what Nikki had done for me that night, I felt like I owed her one.

I pulled off and headed back to the hospital. I stopped by the gift shop and bought Kandi some flowers for her room. I went up to the fourth floor to her room. When I went in, I saw that she had just finished breakfast and Nurse Chauncey was checking her vitals.

"How you feeling?"

Kandi frowned. "Like I had my stomach pumped. Now they are forcing me to eat this nasty food."

"It's not that bad, Candice," Chauncey interjected.

I smiled. "Eat up."

"Well, your *sister* is doing much better, Jasmine," Chauncey said in an ironic tone, letting me know he knew I was lying.

"Thanks."

He turned and looked at Kandi. "Try and get some rest, and a little later I'm gonna come back with Dr. Adams and run a few more tests."

"Okay."

"I'll see ya later, ladies," Chauncey said and walked out of the room.

I went and had a seat in the chair next to her bed.

"You told him you were my sister?" Kandi asked.

"Yeah, guess he let me slide with that one."

"He's cute," Kandi noted.

"Yeah. Anyway, how do you feel?"

Kandi looked away from me. "Like a fool. I know you're disappointed with me."

"I'm more disappointed with myself than you."

"Why? You weren't the one who got fucked up and taken to a hotel by a bunch of niggas."

"No, but I should've been more of a friend to you. I saw the road you were heading down, fucking with Hester and Jade, and I should've stopped you then."

"I should've listened to you."

We sat in silence for a moment, and I listened to the beep of the hospital equipment monitoring Kandi's heart.

"So how long have you known about your heart condition?"

"For about seven years now," she told me.

"So that's why you had an insurance card in your pocketbook."

"Yeah, I have an ACE inhibitor at home to lighten my heart's pumping load and keep it from further enlargement," Kandi explained.

I frowned. "You shouldn't have been dancing at the club in the first place."

"It's okay. I'm supposed to engage in regular exercise anyway. It's good for me. It keeps my heart strong."

"And the cocaine and ecstasy is good for you too?" I quipped. Kandi didn't respond. "Well, that shit ends today. You hear me?"

"Yeah, Jasmine."

"And so does your dancing at The Pink Palace," I added.

Kandi sat up and looked at me. "I can't do that, Jasmine. That's how I'm paying my rent." She shook her head. "I'm already a month behind on it as it is."

"How come you're so behind?"

"Well, when Rayshawn broke up with me, he left me in the apartment, stuck with the rent and all the other bills we had coming in."

"Where are your parents?"

"Florida," she replied. "They think I'm still a student at Clark Atlanta."

"What happened?"

Kandi leaned back in bed. "Well, I'm from St. Petersburg. I got a scholarship to go to Clark, and I fucked up and partied my ass right out of it. My grades slipped and never got back up, and I lost my scholarship. My folks don't know that.

"But I had a plan. That's why I started dancing at The Pink Palace and paying my tuition out of pocket.

I moved in with Rayshawn, and I had it under control, until he left me hanging with the rent and all the other damn bills. Pretty soon I couldn't keep up, and I dropped outta school."

Damn, that was what I did when I was in college, except I was making so much money dancing that after I graduated, I just kept on dancing and making money. I made myself a business. Kandi wasn't so lucky.

"Okay, Kandi, this is what we're going to do: When you get out of here, you're going to move you and your stuff into my condo in Buckhead. Then we're going to get you healthy again, and you're going to get your ass back in school," I told her.

Kandi had a dumbfounded expression on her face. "Jasmine . . . I . . . why are you doing all this?"

"Because you deserve more out of life than this."

Kandi smiled with joy. "I don't know what to say."

"Just say you'll try and do better."

"I will." Kandi paused and then looked at me. "Jasmine, don't take this the wrong way, but what happen between us back at Young Reezy's house party—"

I held up my hand. "We had fun that night, but this is not what this is about. You'll have your own room, and you're free to see whoever you want."

She smiled.

"Now, if you come in drunk one night and climb in my bed, you just might be asking for it."

We both laughed.

"Jasmine, can I ask you something?"

"Sure. What is it?"

"What's your real name? I mean, all this time we've known each other, I've never asked you that."

I grinned. "Well, Candice, my name is Jacqueline Dawson, but only my mother calls me Jacqueline."

"I like that. Your mother lives around here?"

"Smyrna. Her and my father live out there."

"You still talk to them?" she asked.

"My mother, yeah. My father doesn't approve of my lifestyle, so we haven't talked in years really. I could care less about him."

"Oh, my folks would die if they knew I've been dancing at The Pink Palace." She paused and looked at me. "Am I asking you too many questions now?"

"No." I looked at her. "Can I tell you something?"

"Yeah, of course."

"My mother suffered from congestive heart failure three years ago, so when I found out about your condition, it really hit home," I told her. "Scared the hell outta me, actually."

Kandi got a sad expression on her face "I'm sorry, Jasmine." She reached over and hugged me. Wow, I hadn't realized how much I needed that.

"It's okay, Kandi. Now let's get you better, okay?"

Kandi smiled. "Okay."

16

Holding back the years

College Park, GA

NIKKI

I had Penny keep Tyler the night before, and that was a blessing. I hated to admit it, but I'd been keeping my distance from Janelle so she didn't get involved in that shit again, and after seeing Kandi laid up in the hospital, I was glad I had. There was no way I was going to drag her into that mess again.

I picked up Tyler and dropped him off at the daycare center. I headed home, and as soon as I hit my bedroom, my head hit the pillow and I was out.

About six hours later, my phone woke me up out of my sleep, and I saw Polo's name on display. I wondered if he had anything new to tell me.

I accepted his call. "What's up, Polo?"

"Nothing much. I was in your part of town and I wanted to see you. Are you home?"

"Yeah." I sat up in bed. "Come on over."

"Okay. I'll be there in fifteen minutes," he replied.

I got up and went in the shower and freshened myself up. Five minutes later, I got out of the shower and threw on a blue summer dress, went into the kitchen and warmed up some leftover pasta.

I hadn't eaten anything since the day before. After I got a few bites in, I heard my doorbell and I went and opened it and saw Polo. He was of course wearing a red polo shirt, some Ecko Unlimited jeans with a Gucci belt, and a pair of matching Gucci-printed Nikes.

"Hey, Polo," I greeted him and he came in.

"What's going on, Nikki? I heard some shit went down at Reggie's birthday party last night."

I wondered if Reggie had told him about what I did to him. "What they saying?"

"They saying you and Jasmine rolled up on some bitches and regulated they ass. What was that all about?" Polo had a seat on the couch.

I guessed Reggie had decided to keep our little encounter to himself. "Yeah, we did. Some foul shit went down with another one of the girls called Kandi that Hester and Jade could've stopped but didn't. Long story short, Chaz and two other niggas took advantage of Kandi and left her in a bad predicament last night."

"Chaz, that stupid muthafucka that be with Reggie all the time?" Polo said and shook his head. "Figures. Is she all right?"

I sat on the couch next to Polo. "She's at South Fulton, but not really in that good of shape, but not because of what they did. Kandi has some other medical issues."

"Well, I'm glad everything is straight now." Polo looked into my eyes. "I wanted to see you again. You've been on my mind like crazy these past couple of days."

Damn, I had almost forgotten that he said that he loved me the other night. Or maybe I just didn't want to remember it. And here I was in this little dress, fresh out the shower, and he's looking at me like scoop of chocolate ice cream on a sugar cone.

"Polo, I'm not sure we should—"

Polo leaned over and kissed me. I had to admit he was a damn good kisser. His hand touched my bare thigh, and I felt my pussy jump. It had been a minute since I'd been intimate with anybody I was attracted to. The last man I was with was Malachi, and that was torture. He made my skin crawl. The last man that made me feel good was Dre, the man I loved.

Polo's lips tugged at mine with a passion I never knew he had for me. His hand started to move up my thigh, but I stopped him from going farther.

I pulled away from his lips slowly. Dre was still alive, and I was still very much in love with him.

"I can't, Polo."

Polo nodded his head. "It's still too soon, huh? I know you loved Dre, but I don't think he would object to you being happy again, and I can make you very happy, Nikki. That's all I want to do is make you happy."

I leaned back on the couch. "I know you would, Polo, but with everything going on, it's not good timing."

Polo looked at me oddly. "When are you going to have Dre's funeral services? It's been almost a month since he passed."

That question took me off guard. I hadn't even thought about that. I still didn't want to let Polo know the FBI was protecting him

"The coroner's office still has his body, but I'm probably just gonna have a private service for him when they're done."

"Oh, okay. Listen, I'm sorry. I shouldn't be rushing you into anything. I know you're still hurting, and with this bitch-ass nigga Malachi making you dance in his club, I know this is stressful for you."

"Yeah. What are you going to do, Polo? Are you still going to go after him?"

"No doubt. I got a plan in motion right now. Pretty soon that nigga Malachi is going to be served up, and I'll take over his shit," Polo said confidently.

"Well, that's good to hear." I paused and then looked at Polo. "Do you know who Malachi had sent to shoot Dre? Was it Ricky or Reggie?"

Polo shrugged his shoulders. "I don't know who did it, but both of them niggas are going to get the same thing Malachi is going to get, so don't worry about it." He got up and walked to the front door. "You just be careful in that club and let me know if you hear anything I can use."

"I will."

Polo opened the door and walked out to his car out front. As I watched him pull off down the street, I felt bad that I had to continue to lie to him about Dre's condition. He was going to be heartbroken when the truth came out, but I couldn't risk him not following through with his plans to kill Malachi. As long as he was still alive, none of us would be safe.

An hour and a half later, I was out the door to pick Tyler up from the daycare center. I drove up in the parking lot and pulled into a parking space and turned off the engine. Just as I was about to get out of the car, another car pulled up next to me.

"Nikki, I need you to come with me," a familiar voice said.

I looked up, and I couldn't believe my eyes.

JASMINE

The hospital decided to discharge Kandi, and I went to South Fulton to pick her up and take her to her apartment to pick up her things and come back to my condo in Buckhead. It felt good doing this for her. I knew in my heart it was the right thing to do.

There was no way I was going to let her go back to dancing at The Pink Palace. That life was not for her. I knew it the first night I saw her there, but I didn't do the right thing and tell her that. But that was then and this was now.

As I was walking down the smelly hospital hallway, I tried to hold my breath. I couldn't stand the smell. Made me sick!

I saw Nurse Chauncey at the triage desk, and he came out around from it to talk to me.

"So you're here to take Candice home?" he asked.

"Yeah. I'm glad she's doing better."

"She is. Her test came back clean. Just make sure she stays away from all that extra activity at *that club*," he insisted.

I looked at him and smiled. "You don't have to worry about that. I'ma make sure she stays as far away from *that club* as possible. By the way, how do you know about that club?"

Chauncey gave me a sly grin. "Same way I knew you weren't really her sister. Besides, I talked to her and she told me the story. She's lucky Nikki and you found her when y'all did. She could have easily died in that hotel room."

"Oh, well, thank you for letting me be there for her."

He looked me up and down, checking me out, then focused on my eyes. "No problem. She needs all the friends she can get now, and you look like a real good friend."

"I'm trying to be." I turned to head to Kandi's room.

"Before you go, can I ask you something?" Chauncey asked.

I turned back around. "Sure. What's on your mind?"

"Would you mind if I call you sometime? Maybe we could go out somewhere?"

I was taken aback by his offer. I'd never had a man dressed in scrubs ask me for my number before. I usually didn't date men unless I was on the clock, but Nurse Chauncey was very different from the men I usually dealt with—not to mention that he was fine as hell with his big, brown eyes and handsome face.

"I think that would be nice," I replied.

He took out his phone and we exchanged numbers. After he saved my number in his phone, he went and got Kandi a wheelchair.

I walked into Kandi's room, and she was sitting up in bed.

"Hey, Kandi, you ready to go?"

"Very ready," she eagerly replied. "I hate being in hospitals. I need to eat some real food! Plus the smell here is killing me."

I handed her a plastic bag with some clean clothes she could change into. A few minutes later, she was dressed and ready to go. Chauncey came into the room, pushing the wheelchair for Kandi.

"Here we go," Chauncey said and pushed the chair next to the bed for Kandi.

"Do I have to ride in the chair? My legs are fine. I can walk," Kandi protested.

"Hospital policy," he replied.

"C'mon, Kandi. Just get in so we can go. We have a lot of things to take care of," I told her.

She sighed and then sat in the wheelchair. Chauncey smiled at me, and we went down to the hospital lobby. Once outside, Kandi jumped out of the chair, and we laughed.

"You couldn't wait to do that, huh?" Chauncey asked between chuckles.

"You know it," she retorted.

"Well, you take care of yourself, Candice, and I'll call you soon, Jasmine."

I smiled at him. "I'm looking forward to it."

Kandi gave me a surprised look and we walked over to the parking garage to my car.

"You two are going out?"

"Maybe. He asked me for my number, so we'll see what happens."

"Well, he is fine. But I thought you said you only mess with ballers with cash to spend. Chauncey is nice, but he's a nurse. Why the change of heart?" Kandi inquired.

"I don't know. Maybe I'm tired of the same old thing."

17

Daddy's home

College Park, GA

NIKKI

I couldn't believe my eyes when I saw Jayson Harper, Janelle's husband, in the car next to me. I hadn't seen him in months. What was he doing yhere at Tyler's daycare center? Oh my God . . . Tyler!

"Jayson, what are you doing here? Did something happen to Tyler?" I yelled as I jumped out of my car.

"No, no, calm down. Tyler is safe. He's at my house with Janelle, but I need you to come with me now," Jayson said seriously.

Jayson and I had a long history together. When I first met him five years earlier, I knew him by the alias Tommy Holloway. He was running with a nigga named Damien, who I was messing with, as his partner. In actuality, he was an undercover police officer infiltrating the Flip Set drug organization. After I was raped and nearly beaten to death by Damien and his niggas, Jayson was the one who came to my rescue and took me to the hospital. I owed him my life, so I trusted him completely. I quickly jumped in his car.

"What's going on, Jayson? Why does Janelle have Tyler?" I asked him as he pulled out of the parking lot and turned onto the street.

"We just needed him to be somewhere safe."

"Why? Where are we going, Jay?"

He looked at me and smiled. "I'll explain everything once we get there. Trust me."

I nodded my head and sat back. Less than ten minutes later, we were in a neighborhood in Morrow. We pulled up to a house and parked inside the garage.

"Okay, Jayson, what's going on?"

"Come with me," he replied and got out of the car.

I followed him into the house. This was a new house that was empty. *What the hell is going on?* I thought, and then I saw him standing in the living room. My mouth fell open, my heart started rapidly beating, and I couldn't believe my eyes.

"Hey, baby, I've missed you," Dre said.

I ran into his arms. I couldn't even form words at that moment.

"It's okay, Nikki. I'm here now."

"Oh my God . . . How . . . ?"

"Come here, baby. Have a seat," Dre said and took me to the couch.

I looked at him again just to make sure my eyes weren't playing tricks on me, or that this was some kind of illusion. "The FBI? The doctors told me the FBI took you into protective custody."

"That would be me," Jayson spoke up. "I told the hospital to give everybody that story. We needed to get Dre somewhere safe."

"But why? I don't understand." I looked at Dre.

"Okay, babe. Let me explain." Dre took a deep breath then continued. "When I woke up in Emory Hospital, I was as weak as a kitten. I wanted to call you, but I realized that if Malachi knew I was out of my coma, he would send somebody to finish me off, and I couldn't put you and Tyler in danger. I needed to talk to someone I could trust, and the first person I called was Jayson."

Jayson stepped closer. "After Dre got shot, I started to investigate Malachi. I went back to The Pink Palace and started to watch his operation from the inside. Then one night, I saw you walk up in there, and you went straight to Malachi's office. I imagine you came there that night to make a deal with him to spare Dre's life?" he asked, and I confirmed it with a head nod. "I couldn't let you know I was there, so I decided to fall back and watch you. The next thing I knew, you were back dancing at The Pink Palace, and I could tell you weren't happy about that.

"A week later, I got a call from Dre in the hospital, and I filled him in on what was going on."

Dre nodded. "When Jayson told me, I knew that Malachi had eyes on you. So we knew I had to go somewhere safe to recover before we contacted you. I hated it, but I knew it was the right thing to do. Jayson was the only other person I could trust."

"Did Janelle know about this too?" I asked Jayson.

"I just recently told her."

"No offense to you, Jayson"—I looked at Dre—"but why do you keep on saying he was the only person you could trust? What about Polo? He's your best friend."

Dre frowned. "Who do you think shot me in the back?"

"What? But Polo—"

"Is a snake in the grass," Dre said with disgust. "The day in front of the shop when that white Crown Victoria car screeched out in front of me, that punk-ass nigga Reggie was behind the wheel, and that bitch-ass nigga Polo was sitting on the passenger side with a .45 in his hand, pointing it at me."

Once again, my jaw hit the ground. "Oh my God. All this time he's been . . . Dre, I know why he did it."

"I do too. So he could get rid of me so he could get to you."

I grew even more disgusted with Polo than I was with Malachi. "That fucking traitor! I can't believe I felt sorry for him. I'm going to kill him!"

Dre caressed my face. "Not before I do."

I looked at Jayson. "I mean it, Jayson. You can arrest me now, 'cause he's a dead man."

Jayson nodded. "I understand how you feel. Believe me, I do. What we're doing here now is completely off the books. I owe Dre this after what he did for Janelle back when." Jayson was referring to Dre killing Damien, my crazy ex-lover, after he went after her and almost raped Janelle three years ago. "But Malachi isn't going to rest until Dre is dead."

"Polo is going after him too," I informed them.

"How do you know? Last time we checked, Polo was trying to get down with his crew," Dre inquired.

"He's Don P. He's the one that sent those killers after Malachi in Lenox Mall."

"What? He's Don P," Jayson said, stunned. "We've been trying to figure out for weeks who was behind that hit. And everybody has been trying to find out who Don P is on the streets."

"He told me everything. He even wants me to give him information about when Malachi is most vulnerable so he can take him out," I told them.

"We can use this to our advantage," Jayson said to Dre.

"Yeah, we can," he confirmed.

I stared at Dre. "Are you sure you're okay? You lost so much blood."

"I was in a lot of fucking pain, and I've been popping painkillers like Tic Tacs. I was lucky the bullet hit nothing vital. Once I got here and started rehabbing with a friend Jayson brought over, I started to gain my strength back. Jayson has been keeping me off of the police radar for the past month."

"I'ma give you guys some time to catch up. Janelle and I will keep Tyler at our place tonight," Jayson told us.

"Thanks, man."

I got up and hugged Jayson. "Thank you for taking care of Dre."

"That's what family is for," he replied. "I'll be back in the morning," Jayson said and went to the garage and pulled out in his car.

I still couldn't believe this was happening. I was there with Dre, and he was okay.

"I've missed you so much," I said to him.

"Not as much as I've missed you, baby," Dre replied and hugged me tight. "It's been torture knowing you were back in The Pink Palace dancing for that nigga."

"I'm so sorry, baby," I said, breaking down in tears. "I . . . had to."

"Ssshh. You don't have to tell me. I know you were trying to protect me. But I'm here now, and I'm going to protect you now."

I kissed him with all the passion and love I had inside me. Dre pulled off my jacket and kissed my neck. My pussy instantly became moist, feeling his lips on my soft spot as his big, strong hands caressed my body. He pulled down the straps of my dress, and it dropped to the floor. Dre stared at my body then picked me up and carried me to the bedroom and laid me on the bed.

We spent the next few hours making love like we never had before, and for the first time in weeks, I felt whole.

JASMINE

After we picked up Kandi's clothes and a few items from her apartment, I settled her into a room in my condo. She was so blown away by the size of my place and all of the amenities. We ordered a pizza and watched DVDs most of the night, until she was tired and went to bed. She may not have wanted to admit it, but she still needed some more rest after her binge Sunday night.

The next day, I took her grocery and clothing shopping. To be honest, most of the clothes she had from her old apartment weren't worth keeping. I wanted her to have a new look and a fresh start before she went back to Clark. Later on that week, we would go down to the campus and get her registered for classes that fall. I was going to make sure she stayed on course this time around.

As we were shopping at Old Navy in Buckhead Station, my phone started to play Ludacris's "My Chick Bad," and I saw Chauncey's name illuminate on the display.

"Hello," I said playfully.

"Hey, Jasmine. How are you doing?"

"I'm doing good."

"How's Candice?" he inquired.

"She's doing good. She's here with me, and we're doing a little retail therapy."

"Sounds like fun." He paused then continued. "Listen, I was wondering if you'd like to go out for drinks tonight."

I smiled. "Where?"

"The Apache Club. We can hear a little jazz, drink a little something, and get to know each other a little better," he said.

"Sounds like fun."

"So can I pick you up?"

I hesitated for a moment. I didn't tell dudes where I lived. "Ah, how about I pick you up instead?" I asked.

"Ah, sure. That's fine," Chauncey replied.

After he gave me his address, I hung up and finished shopping with Kandi.

Later that night, we stopped at Chipotle and got some food and headed home. It was time for me to get dressed, and I was feeling excited. It was weird, because I hadn't been on a real date with a man in years. I'd been so caught up in dancing and making money that I didn't even miss dating for fun. Besides, I was fucking niggas who was giving me so much cash I didn't care if it wasn't a real date.

I decided to wear a black BCBG dress with a single twisted strap over my left shoulder. It had a pleated waist with side-knotted detail at the waist. I wore my hair down, with a little MAC makeup on my face.

I walked out of my bedroom, and Kandi saw me and smiled. "Damn, don't you look good! Poor Chauncey ain't going to know what to do with himself," she affirmed.

"Well, he better figure it out," I quipped. "Don't wait up."

I walked out the front door and to my car. Once inside, I put Chauncey's address into my GPS and took off.

Once I arrived at his house over on Lynn Avenue, I parked in the driveway and walked up to his front door. I could feel the butterflies in my stomach. Damn, this felt like a real first date.

I rang his doorbell, and a few seconds later, Chauncey opened the door. He looked so damn handsome. This was my first time seeing him outside of his scrubs, and boy did he clean up well. He was wearing a white button-down shirt with black jeans and black loafers. The scent of his Vera Wang cologne filled my nostrils, and I was turned on by him.

"Wow. You look great," he droned, as he looked me up and down.

"You don't look half bad yourself, Nurse Chauncey."

He grinned. "I'm off the clock. You can just call me Chauncey."

"Cool. Are you ready to go?"

"Anywhere with you," he replied.

We got in my car, and I jumped on I-20 West to midtown.

It had been a while since I'd been to the Apache Club, but after a couple of wrong turns, we found the little club in the cut near the Varsity. We went inside, and it was pretty much the same as I remembered. It was dimly lit, with a live band playing in the front. It was a very eclectic club that had a gallery of erotic S&M pictures and paintings on the walls.

Chauncey checked us in, and we found a small table in the back. After the waitress took our drink orders, Chauncey and I listened to the band on stage play a few sets. The waitress returned with my Long Island Iced Tea and his Hypnotiq and grapefruit juice.

"They're good," I insisted to Chauncey.

"Yeah, they got a real original style. Kinda like you," he flirted.

"And what do you know about my style?"

"I've learned quite a bit about you."

I raised my eyebrow. "Like what?"

"Well, I see you have quite a following on Facebook." He laughed.

"I guess I do. So, are you a fan?"

"You didn't get my friend request?" he quipped.

I laughed. "What else do you know about me?"

Chauncey stared at me and then took a sip of his drink. "Well, it appears that you're an exotic dancer at The Pink Palace. You have calendars and posters for sale on your Web site. And you're a registered Democrat, according to your Facebook page."

I sipped on my iced tea. "Did you know all this before you asked me for my number?"

"No, I didn't."

I started to feel weird, sitting there with him like he didn't know what type of chick I was. "Did you also go to The Pink Palace to watch me dance? Throw a couple of dollars on the stage?"

"I don't really do strip clubs."

I chuckled. "You don't? Why not?"

"Well, to me it's kind of like going to a restaurant and watching them cook a nice, big, juicy steak and not being able to eat it. If I wanna tease myself, I'll just buy some porn," he joked, but I didn't laugh. "What's wrong?"

"I'm just wondering, why did you ask me out in the first place? I'm not exactly your type."

"And how do you know what's my type?" he asked.

I sighed. "You're in the medical field. I'm sure you have dozens of nurses, doctors, and interns you can ask out. You're not an ugly man."

"Thank you. That's true, but why don't you think I would date somebody like you?"

I rolled my eyes. "You don't even know who I am."

"But that's the reason why we're both here—to get to know each other."

"Really? Sounds like you know everything already."

"Do you always try to sabotage the dates you go on?" he joked.

I took a swig of my drink. "Okay, you wanna get to know me? The real me?"

"I'm dying to."

"Okay, let's put it all on the table. I'm a stripper."

"I already knew that," he quipped.

"I dance for money."

"Isn't that by definition what a stripper does?"

"I normally don't fuck with guys like you. If you don't have money, I don't have time for you."

He grinned. "But yet you're here with me, so I'm doing something right."

"I'm bisexual."

"Well, that's great, 'cause I like girls too."

I smirked. "I fuck for money, if the price is right."

Chauncey sipped his drink. "After we have sex, you'll pay me."

Okay, I wasn't expecting that little come back. I took another sip of my drink.

"Is that it? Is it my turn now," he asked.

I shrugged my shoulders. "I'm a male nurse. I like my job. I was born and raised in North Philly by my grandparents. My mother died when I was six. Cancer. I never really knew my father. I saw him like three times a year or on holidays. He was a bit of a crack-head, clean one week then a fiend the next. I moved to Atlanta last year, and I rent my house. I haven't met a woman that has really interested me enough to date more than once or twice until this past Sunday night."

Okay, I felt like an ass now. He liked me despite my lifestyle. "Oh, thanks. So you became a nurse because of your mother?"

"Sorta. I was going to become a doctor, but I really enjoyed talking and helping the patients more than just trying to fix them. I'm a people person.

"So, you're more than just a stripper. You're like a mini mogul. I imagine you make lots of money merchandising yourself like that. You got a real business mind."

I smiled at him for acknowledging my business hustle. Most men only saw my tits and ass and thought I had nothing else going for me in life.

"Well, I did graduate from Spelman with a bachelor's degree, so I might as well put all that hard work to use."

"Smart and sexy. You're a rare breed, Jasmine."

"You're pretty remarkable yourself, Chauncey."

The waitress returned and we ordered another round of drinks and continued to get to know each other. We started to talk about everything from politics to music, and I found myself digging this man's mind just as much as I did his body. Chauncey was a great guy, not to mention sexy as hell, and the more we talked and drank, the hornier I became.

The next thing we knew it was two o'clock in the morning, and we decided to head out. I drove Chauncey back to his house and pulled up in his driveway.

"Well, maybe next time I can pick you up," Chauncey joked.

"Yeah, maybe next time you will," I confirmed.

Chauncey smiled and leaned over and kissed me softly, and my pussy started to dance. Wow. He pulled away and opened his car door.

"I know this is usually the other way around, but you know . . . since you picked me up for this date and you're taking me home . . ." Chauncey rambled. "Anyway, do you wanna come in for a nightcap?"

I stared at his fine ass for a second and pictured him with no clothes on, "Yeah, I'd love a nightcap."

We got out of the car and walked to his front door. Chauncey fumbled with his keys until he found the right one and opened his door.

He flipped on the lights and turned around, took my shawl from me, and hung it on his coat hanger. He turned and looked at me, and I grabbed him by his shirt and pulled him closer to me. Our tongues danced with each other.

"What about the nightcap?" he asked.

"Fuck it. I'll drink it in the morning," I said and kissed him again.

Chauncey took me to his bedroom. We fumbled and moved around his bedroom until we reached his bed. Chauncey pulled my twisted strap down over my left shoulder, and my dress hit the floor.

I stood there in my Victoria's Secret black lace bra and panties and then Chauncey turnede me around to undo my bra, letting it join my dress on the floor. His hands cupped my soft titties as he kissed my neck. My pussy was dripping with excitement.

I turned around and unzipped his jeans as he unbuttoned his shirt. I wanted him so bad, more than any man I'd been with in a long time. My hands found his manhood, and it felt like he was swinging a baseball bat between his thighs.

I sat on the bed behind me and pulled his jeans and boxers down, and his long, thick dick popped up in front of my face. I licked his swollen mushroom head like a lollipop before I took him to the back of my throat.

Chauncey threw his head back as I had my way with him, sucking the skin off his juicy stick. He placed one hand under my jaw and the other behind my head, and moved his member in and out of my mouth. He tasted so good.

He soon pulled out before he released his seeds in my mouth and pushed me back on his bed. Then he licked my neck and traced his tongue down my chest to my rock-hard nipples. He sucked the left then the right, then continued his journey down south. He dropped to his knees as his tongue licked my belly.

Chauncey licked me down my inner thighs, making my pussy jealous. My was pussy was trickling with cream, and soon he tasted my flavor. He pushed my legs apart, giving himself plenty of room to enjoy his meal. If I hadn't known better, I would have sworn that Chauncey was an OB/GYN instead of a nurse, 'cause he knew my pussy like he'd been there before.

The sounds of my moans echoed in his room as I rode the waves of an orgasm.

Chauncey stood up, went into the nightstand next to his bed, and pulled out a condom. He ripped it open, stroked his hardness, and then rolled the condom on. He then climbed on top and kissed me. I was not used to so much kissing, but damn, I liked it.

He then pushed his dick into my creamy tunnel, and I clamped down on his thickness. Most men just started pumping and fucking the shit outta me at this point, but Chauncey took his time and grinded against my pussy, making me cream even more.

I wrapped my legs behind his back, keeping him deep in me. He sucked my neck; I scratched his back and sang his name like I was recording a demo. Most of the time I faked shit just to stroke a nigga's ego, but the way Chauncey was stroking my pussy was driving me crazy.

He pulled out of my wetness, and I begged for him to put it back. Me, begging, was totally unheard of, but there I was, begging for his dick.

Chauncey grinned and turned me over flat on my stomach. He spread my legs apart and re-entered my pussy from the back. This time, he groaned like a beast. He lay on my back and then gave me the business.

I demanded that he fuck me, as I pushed my ass back at him. His stomach clapped against my ass, giving us the applause we deserved for our performance. There was no rest for us that night.

The morning came, and I was wrapped in Chauncey's arms, exhausted and ecstatic from our lovemaking. My hair was a mess. His bed was soaked.

I stared at Chauncey and smiled. "Okay, you were right. How much do I owe you?"

He smiled. "Don't worry. I'ma start a tab."

"Cool. My credit is good."

"But you're sex is better," Chauncey added.

I snuggled my head in his chest. "And you're incredible."

"You seduced me."

"You invited me in. I'll take that nightcap now."

"I got you." He laughed and caressed my ass, and it felt so good.

I didn't wanna fool myself into thinking this was going to be any more than what it was, so I didn't say anymore. Still, all this time I thought I would never meet a man who could make me feel so good was now thrown out the window.

18

The business

Atlanta, GA

MALACHI

I had finally worked out the details of my deal with Carlos, my new connect out of Miami. This was vital for me to keep my grip on the streets. Ricky was picking up my first shipment that day.

I was still on guard and looking to find this Don P before he tried again to kill me. Not knowing who that pussyhole was made me paranoid. I couldn't trust anybody. I never had before, but now I couldn't put anything past anybody.

I sent Latoya and Courtney to New Orleans to stay with her parents. I didn't need them to be in the line of fire again. Plus, now was the perfect time to bring sweet Nikki into my world completely. It was time to put her in her place and make her my woman. I needed to taste that sweet pussy again. No need to pretend any longer that she had a choice in the matter.

My phone rang. "What is it?"

"Jasmine wants to come up and see you, boss," Bump replied.

She probably wanted some cash for ass. That was okay. My dick needed to feel some tight pussy anyway.

"Send her up."

"Okay," Bump replied and hung up.

A few seconds later, he brought her up to my office.

Jasmine was dressed in jeans and a T-shirt, not ready to work but maybe just there to fuck. I loved the way that bitch worked. She was always on her hustle.

"Hello, sweet Jasmine. You needed to see me?"

Jasmine smiled and sat in the chair in front of my desk. "As a matter of fact, I do."

"About business or pleasure?"

"Everything is business, Malachi, but I need to talk to you about one of the little niggas in your crew," she clarified.

"Another one of them niggas getting rude with the girls?"

"Worse. The other night at Reggie's party here, that nigga Chaz and two others took a girl name Kandi up out of here. She was high and fucked up. They took her to a hotel, and she nearly ODed. They just left her there to die," Jasmine explained.

"Is the bitch dead?"

She frowned. "No, she's not, but if Nikki and I hadn't got to her in time, she would be."

"Nikki and you? You two spending time together now?" I asked.

"Not really, but she was the one who called me and told me what Chaz and them were doing to her."

"I heard Nikki put on a good show for Reggie. You like her?"

"Malachi, what does that have to do with anything? Didn't you hear what I said? Chaz left Kandi to die in a sleazy hotel room," she said, upset.

I shrugged my shoulders. "What do you want me to do about it?"

Jasmine leaned forward in the chair. "Fuck that nigga up!"

"For what? If these bitches want to get high and kill themselves, I can't help that. As long as her ass doesn't die in my club, I don't give a damn."

Jasmine stood up. "Really? So that's it? You don't give a fuck?"

I didn't respond, 'cause I didn't care.

"All you care about up in here is Nikki." She chuckled. "Then I suggest you check your stupid little brother."

I glared at her. "What does that mean?"

She walked to the door then turned around. "It means he tried to take some pussy from your number one bitch in the locker room Sunday night. Guess he's trying to be like you. Still don't give a damn?"

Jasmine walked out, and I turned around in my chair and saw Reggie sitting at a booth, getting a lap dance. My blood boiled looking at his dumb ass. I told that asshole to stay away from her, and he pulled that?

I got up and marched downstairs. Bump followed behind me. I walked up to Reggie in the booth with the bitch in his lap.

"Get the fuck up," I said to the bitch, and she jumped up.

"Dang, bruh, I was just getting a little bull ride," he said happily.

I slapped the shit out of him. Reggie fell back in the booth. "Mal! What you do that for?"

I started punching the shit out of him as he tried to cover himself. Reggie fell on the ground, and I started to kick him. I grabbed a beer bottle from the table and busted it over his head. Blood ran down his face.

"Malachi, please? No more!"

"I told you not to touch her. If you weren't my brother, I would kill you right now." I glared at him, "Go clean yourself up."

Everybody in the club stared at me with fear. Good. I stared back at them, and they all went back to their business. I had to set an example for them all. Not even my brother could disobey me and not suffer. Now I had to go check on Nikki and make sure she knew that my word was law.

NIKKI

Waking up in Dre's arms was the best feeling in the world. We had spent the night making love until we couldn't move. A few hours later, Jayson called and said he was on his way back over with Janelle and Tyler.

The garage door opened, and Jayson parked inside; then we heard the side door open, and in walked Janelle, carrying Tyler in her arms. His little eyes lit up when he saw his daddy standing in front of him. He reaches his little arms toward him.

"Daddy!"

"Hey there, big man! You miss Daddy?" Dre asked.

Tyler hugged him tight and nodded his head. I'd never seen Tyler so happy in his life. He was his father's son for real.

Dre exhaled and held on to his son, just as happy as Tyler was. I hugged them both, and for the first time in months, our family was whole.

After Dre spent a few hours playing with Tyler, I put him down for a nap in the bedroom, and all four of us sat in the living room and tried and figure out our next move.

"I didn't realize how much I missed him," Dre said happily.

"He's missed you too," Janelle added.

Jayson got up and walked to the window and peeped outside.

"Who's place is this, Jayson?" I asked him.

"It's a safe house we use to protect witnesses before trial. It was currently not being used, and it was perfect for us," he enlightened me. "Now, you say Polo is gunning for Malachi?"

"Yes. He's going by the name Don P."

"Hmm." Jayson turned and looked at Dre. "As much as you hate Polo, we may be able to use him to take care of Malachi. I know you wanna kill him, but murdering him in cold blood on the streets is going to bring police attention to you, and I can't protect you from that."

Dre leaned back on the couch. "I know that. I've been thinking the same thing too. If we can get them to go after each other, that would be perfect. Either Polo will kill Malachi, or he'll kill Polo. Or they'll kill each other."

"But how do you get them to do that?" Janelle asked.

"We tell Malachi who Polo is," I told her.

"Not you," Dre said firmly. "You're not setting a foot back in that club."

"Besides, Malachi would be suspicious of that information coming from you," Jayson added.

I smiled. "I may have a way of letting him find out from a source he would trust."

"Who?"

"This girl that works at the club called Jasmine. She's Malachi number one moneymaker, and she's real close to him."

"But can you trust her?" Dre asked.

"We've gotten close, and I think if I can show her the benefit for her in doing this for me, she will."

Jayson folded his arms. "I don't know. It sounds too risky. I've seen Jasmine at the club, and she's the type that only makes moves if it makes money for her. I think if we can tie Malachi to the shootout at Lenox, that might be a better way to take him down."

"But it doesn't solve our problem with Polo," I pointed out. "Trust me, Jayson, I know what type of woman Jasmine is. I used to be just like her. I know how to get through to her."

"Are you sure you can trust her?" Dre asked again.

"I'm sure. This is the best way we can solve all of our problems without directly putting ourselves at risk."

"Okay, I trust you," Dre confirmed.

"If you say you can do it then I believe you," Janelle adds.

Jayson was still thinking it over. He, more than any one of us, knew the danger involved in playing both sides of the fence. He had been deep cover for eight months, infiltrating the Flip Set clique. Somebody also betrayed him that he thought he could trust, and he took a bullet because of it, so he knew what was at stake.

"Okay, we'll do it, but no direct contact with Malachi. I will be following you when you make contact with Jasmine."

"That's fine."

"Okay, so let's figure out where and when this will all go down," Jayson said.

For the next few hours, we all discussed and planned how we would take both of these fools down and get away with it. Once we decided on a course of action, Janelle and Jayson decided to give Dre, Tyler, and me some more time alone.

It felt like it had been years since we'd all been together like that. I had felt like my family and life were forever ruined because of this mess, and now I realized I would do anything to protect the ones I loved.

Dre looked at me sitting on the couch. "So are you still going to marry me?"

"There's nothing more I want to do. I still have the ring at home. I had to take it off because—"

"I know. We've been through so much bullshit over the years." He shook his head. "You did what you had to do for us, Nikki, so I'm going to also do the same. I love you."

I leaned over and kissed his lips. "I love you too." I pulled out my phone. "I guess it's time to set things up," I said and dialed Jasmine's number. After the second ring she answered.

"Hey, Nikki. What's up?"

"Hey, Jasmine, I need to talk to you about something very important."

"Okay. Like I said, if you need help, just ask," Jasmine affirmed.

"Can I meet you somewhere and talk?"

"Sure. Where?"

"How about the bookstore in midtown on Ponce De Leon in about an hour?" I suggested.

"Sounds good. I'll see you then," she said and ended the call.

I looked at Dre. "Everything is all set up. Jayson said he'll be blending in with the shoppers. They're waiting for us."

"Okay, babe. I trust you."

As if on cue, my phone started to ring, and I saw Malachi's name on the display.

"It's Malachi."

Dre scowled. "This nigga got nerve. Answer it."

"What the hell do you want?" I said when I answered.

"My dear Nikki, I've been missing you," Malachi replied.

"I don't give a damn."

"I've warned you about your mouth. You need to learn to listen, or I'll have to teach you too," he said callously.

"And you need to learn when to fuck off. I'm done dancing for you. You and that club can kiss my ass!"

"You're trying my patience, Nikki. Get your ass to this club now, or there will be consequences for your actions—things that once I start, I won't stop until you learn," Malachi warned me menacingly.

I rolled my eyes. "Save your threats for someone who gives a damn. You come after me, and I got something for that ass, nigga! So go eat a dick and stay the hell away from me," I yelled and hung up on his ass.

Dre smiled and clapped his hands. "I couldn't have said it better myself."

19

A common enemy

Midtown Atlanta, GA

JASMINE

After my chat with Malachi, I had lost all respect for that nigga. I'd always had a certain level of respect for him more than anybody else there. After all, he was the head nigga in charge. I understood that he was a gangster and not a gentleman, especially when it came to our business transactions. He paid me top dollar to dance at The Pink Palace and for sex. We never pretended it was anything other than that. But that bullshit he said about not giving a damn about any bitch in his club really pissed me off. At that moment, he became another trick in my eyes, and I was done fucking with him. I could go dance at Magic City, Strokers, or The Pink Pony South and make just as much money, if not more.

I was glad I had told him what his nasty little brother was trying to do to Nikki. He needed his ass kicked.

I was surprised to get a call from Nikki, asking me to meet her at the bookstore in midtown. I knew whatever it was she wanted to discuss had to be important. I'd been dying for months to know what was going on between Malachi and her, and I just might find out.

I walked into the bookstore and saw folks browsing around. I even spotted the new Eric Jerome Dickey novel in his Gideon series that I wanted to read. I would have to remember to pick it up on the way out. I then spotted Nikki sitting by herself at a table in the Seattle Coffee section, waiting for me. She was sipping on a coffee when I walked over to her.

"I hope you weren't waiting long for me," I said and had a seat at the table.

"Naw, I just got here a few minutes ago myself. I love the coffee here. By the way, how's Kandi?"

"She's actually doing much better. I moved her in with me a few days ago."

Nikki's eyebrows rose. "Really? I guess you were serious about trying to be a friend to her."

"Yeah, she needs good people around her now. I'm not exactly sure if I'm that person, but I'm all she got. Her days of dancing at The Pink Palace are done. I'm going to make sure she gets back in Clark and finish her education."

"I have a feeling Kandi is in good hands," Nikki confirmed.

"So what's up, Nikki? Why do you need to speak to me?"

Nikki took another sip of her coffee and then put it on the table. "Well, I have a serious problem with Malachi, and I need your help to solve it."

I folded my legs under the table and leaned back in my chair. "I know there's something going on between you two, but you've never wanted to talk about it before. Why now?"

"Things have change for me. I've found a way from up under his thumb permanently," Nikki said seriously.

"Okay, I need you to explain it to me. Everything."

Nikki sighed and looked at the table then back at me. "All right. If I'm going to ask you for your help, I might as well tell you the truth." She paused momentarily and gathered her thoughts. "My fiancé, the father of my child, Dre, used to do business with Malachi a few years ago. This was before Malachi owned The Pink Palace."

"Back in the day when you used to dance there?"

"Correct. Dre was getting his supply from Malachi, but when he got arrested, the police took his supply and he took a big loss. Fortunately, Dre had some great lawyers on his case, and he was able to beat a lot of the charges he was facing and only did a year in prison.

"When he got out, he was done with the drug game, and I was done with my life at The Pink Palace, and we had a son together. Unfortunately, Dre still owed Malachi a lot of money, but Dre was able to make a deal to pay him back his money over a period of time."

"Let me guess. Once Dre paid him back what he owed him, Malachi still wanted more," I presumed.

"Yeah, he wanted more, but Dre wasn't going to pay him. So Malachi had Dre shot right in front of my baby and me," Nikki said.

"Damn. I'm sorry, Nikki."

"It's okay. Dre didn't die. He fell into a coma, and by this time, I was desperate to do anything to stop Malachi from finishing the job he had already started. So I went to him and made a deal."

"That was the night I saw you walk up in the club and head straight for his office. I was wondering who the hell you were and why Malachi let you in," I said and chuckled to myself.

"Yeah . . . that night. That dirty muthafucka said that if I danced in The Pink Palace, I could 'work' off the debt Dre owed him. But I knew this sick bastard just wanted me up in there for his enjoyment."

"That explains so much, like why you never wanted to be there."

She nodded her head.

"So what's changed now?" I asked.

Nikki sighed. "Dre's awake now. He's been awake for weeks now, getting better, and I've been lying to Malachi, saying that he's dead."

"Shit. That's a dangerous game you're playing, Nikki. So why don't you all just get the fuck outta town?"

"'Cause there's another problem. The nigga who shot Dre was also his best friend, Polo."

My mind searched my memory banks instantly. "Polo, that nigga that's always with Reggie? That's Dre's best friend? Why would he stab his boy in the back like that?"

"Because of me. Polo said that he's been in love with me for years. I guess he saw his chance to get rid of Dre and get at me."

I smiled. "Well, aren't you just little Miss Popular? Does Polo know Dre's alive?"

"No. He's held up somewhere safe right now."

"This is a hell of a shithole you got yourself into, Nikki, but I don't see how I can help you."

Nikki leaned in closer to the table. "Would you help me?"

"If I could, yeah."

"Why?"

"Because I can't stand Malachi's ass," I said frankly.

"Wow, I kinda thought you two had something going on."

I rolled my eyes. "That was strictly business, and I'm done fucking with his ass on that tip. After what happened to Kandi and him telling me he didn't give a shit, that just told me it's time to move the fuck on."

"I could've told you that a long time ago," she said and laughed.

"Yeah . . . so why do you feel like you can trust me all of a sudden?"

Nikki looked into my eyes. "I don't know. Maybe because I feel like in some ways when I look at you, I see a lot of myself. I think you see that too."

"I hate to admit it, but I do too. I see you, and I wonder what my future is going to be. It's just weird."

"Jasmine, your future is whatever you want it to be. Besides, where you are with your game, I never was. You have a business mind like I've never seen in a bitch," Nikki joked.

"Why, thank you," I said with a smile. "But getting back to my question: What makes you think I can help you?"

"Well, you know this beef that Malachi is having with this Don P nigga?"

"Yeah, Malachi is so uptight about it, he ain't going nowhere unless he's thirty deep."

Nikki picked up her coffee and sipped it. "What if I told you I know who that nigga Don P is? How much money do you think Malachi will pay for that information?"

I uncrossed my legs and leaned forward on the table. "A nice penny or two. You're saying you know who he is? But how does that help you with your situation?"

She narrowed her eyes. "Because that foul-ass nigga Polo is Don P."

"What!"

"Yep. So we have a plan to set them fools up. We just need somebody who Malachi would trust to deliver that info."

I grinned. "Oh, I get it. So they can take each other out for you. That is brilliant."

"And it can also be profitable for you. Malachi would pay top dollar to find this shit out," she said.

"Yes, he would. But you know what?"

"What?"

"I would do it for free if it meant getting rid of Malachi."

Nikki laughed and took my hand. "But the cash is just an extra motivator!"

"Exactly," I confirmed and laughed with her. "So what do you need me to do?"

After Nikki explained the plan Dre and her had come up with to eliminate both Malachi and Polo, we parted ways and I headed home. This was a dangerous game I was about to play, but it was also worth it. I couldn't believe the story Nikki told me about what that foul-ass nigga Malachi had done to her, and I was even more shocked about what she said about that lame-ass nigga Polo. I'd always seen him around Reggie, hanging out at The Pink Palace looking shifty. He always gave me a bad vibe, and now I knew why. That snake shot his own best friend to get at his woman. How foul can you get?

The plan that Nikki came up with was airtight, and we were going to set it off that Saturday night. I just needed to get Malachi to believe my story, and I would get paid in the meantime. Maybe a cool $25,000 or even $50,000. He would pay for what I knew. Even if things went bad and Malachi survived the setup, I would still be in the clear with the money. I just hoped he caught a hot one between his eyes for all the pain he'd caused Nikki and her family.

I was also excited about that night as well. Chauncey was coming over to my place for dinner. It was the first time I'd ever brought a man back to my condo.

I didn't know what it was, but there was something about him I found simply irresistible, not to mention arousing! This was the first time in a long time I'd found myself so drawn to a man. He excited me not only physically but mentally too. I couldn't believe out of all the niggas I'd fucked with—ballers, athletes, and gangsters—that I was dating a male nurse, of all people. This was crazy for me.

I soon reached home. I looked at my watch and it was 5:30 p.m. Chauncey said he'd be over at 8:00, so that gave me just under three hours to cook and get ready for dinner.

I went inside and saw that Kandi had already started dinner for me. She was such a sweet girl.

"Hey, Jasmine! You're running behind schedule for your date," she noted.

"I know. Thanks for starting dinner for me."

Kandi giggled. "No problemo! Besides, I'm glad you hit it off with Nurse Chauncey," she teased.

I walked into the kitchen and opened the oven. The beef flanks were cooking very well. "Don't call him that when he gets here."

"Okay! I just can't believe you two are on a second date. He must have really put it on you the other night," Kandi said and put her finger in her mouth seductively.

I couldn't help but smile at her sexy ass. If I wasn't feeling Chauncey so much, I might have had to seduce her again. "Yes, he did. And he's gonna put it on me again tonight!"

"Ooohhh, mind if I watch?" Kandi inquired playfully.

"You know me. I don't give a damn. 'Cause I know you gonna hear some moaning and groaning tonight," I insisted.

Kandi laughed hard, and so did I, 'cause we both knew I wasn't lying.

I headed to my room and picked out my clothes for dinner. I was going to wear a blue mini wrap dress by Michael Kors and matching blue Chanel shoes. I wanted to feel sexy that night, so I went and ran the water in my tub for a Tokyo Milk bubble bath.

After an hour of soaking my body in the soothing bath solution, I got up and got dressed. I decided to wear my hair up to show off my neck. Chauncey loved sucking on it, so I wanted to tease him all night. By the time I got done fixing my hair and applying my makeup, I heard my doorbell chime. It was 8:00 on the dot. Chauncey was prompt.

I heard Kandi open the door for him, and he was happy to see her. I stepped out of my room looking fierce, and once again his eyes lit up when he saw me.

"Wow, I feel underdressed now," Chauncey said referring to his red Avirex shirt and matching black jeans.

"Not at all. I just wanted to look good for you tonight," I said to him.

"I don't think you couldn't," Chauncey droned and walked over to me.

Kandi winked at me and licked her lips behind his back, letting me know Chauncey looked fine as fuck. I winked back, acknowledging her.

"Are you hungry?"

Chauncey grinned and looked me up and down "Very."

"For food," I smirked and clarified.

"Yeah, whatever that is you got in there smells good."

"Why, thank you," Kandi said.

I cut my eyes at her. I wanted him to think I cooked it.

Chauncey laughed. "So you didn't cook, huh?"

"I was running late, and Kandi was nice enough to start it for me."

"And finish it," he added.

I rolled my eyes. "Details."

I led him to the living room, and he had a seat.

"This is a real nice place you got here, Jasmine. Like something outta *MTV Cribs*," he joked.

"It cozy."

"Well, I'll put dinner on the table for you and give you two some privacy," Kandi told us.

"Thank you," I said, and she disappeared into the kitchen.

"I'm glad to see she's doing better. I knew you would take good care of her," Chauncey affirmed.

"I'm trying," I sat down next to him. "I'm glad you came over. I don't normally invite men over here."

"Then I feel special to be the first."

"You should," I joked, and Chauncey leaned over and kissed me. Damn, I could feel myself getting so wet. What was this man doing to me?

We heard Kandi clear her throat. "Dinner is on the table, y'all."

"Thank you, Kandi."

"I'll be in my room," she crooned and bounced off.

We both moved to the dining room and had a seat. Damn, Kandi did her thing. Beef flank, roasted potatoes, and collard greens sat on the table in front of us. If I knew she could cook like this, I would have moved her in a long time ago!

Chauncey picked up the bottle of Moscato and the corkscrew. He opened the bottle and poured us both a glass into the champagne flutes.

"Can I make a toast?" he asked.

"Sure."

"To getting to know each other even better," he said and we drank to that.

We both dug into our food, and man, it was good. Kandi should have become a chef instead of a stripper.

After dinner we went to the couch, and I turned on the stereo. R. Kelly and Keri Hilson's "Number One Sex" started to play in the background.

"Let me ask you something, Jasmine. Where do you see yourself in five years?"

I thought about that. "I want to own a business, something in the entertainment field. I haven't really mapped it out yet."

"Maybe you should start," he replied.

"I got a question for you."

He smiled. "Shoot."

"Why are you still dating me after I told you what my lifestyle is like?"

"I like you. A lot."

"Seriously. I'm not the type of girl you bring home to your momma."

"My momma is dead, remember?" he said.

"Sorry." I shook my head. "I shouldn't have said that."

"Relax. Listen, I don't like to judge people until I get to know them. And from what I've learned from being around you, you're a funny, sexy, smart, and caring woman. All the things I like in a woman, Jasmine," he said and touched my face.

"Jacqueline. My real name is Jacqueline." I didn't know why I just told him that. It just felt right.

"Jacqueline? I like that," he said and kissed my lips.

I couldn't believe it. I might have been falling for this guy. How the hell did that happen? One day I was "Money Over Niggas," the next thing I knew I was dating the night nurse. Whatever, this felt right, and so did the way he was touching my leg.

His hands traveled further up my thick chocolate thigh, until he was under my dress and he touched my fire.

He pulled away. "You're not wearing any panties."

"Hmmm, I must have forgot to put them on," I said and smiled.

Chauncey kissed me again and put his thumb on my swollen clit and rubbed me the right way.

"Aahh," I moaned, and it felt like a river flowing between my thighs.

Chauncey inserted his index finger into my tight hole, and I grinded on his fingers. My hand caressed his dick in his jeans, and he was harder than a brick. I unzipped his fly and pulled out his beautiful, long dick and gripped it and rubbed it up and down.

Chauncey groaned as I stroked his manhood. I couldn't take anymore, and I decided to straddle him right there on the couch. Chauncey let out a lustful hiss as I slid down his meaty shaft. My dress was bunched up around my waist, exposing my fat ass as I ponied up and down his dick, driving him crazy.

R. Kelly's "Echo" was providing the soundtrack to our lust. As we were getting our freak on, I spied Kandi poking her head out of her room down the hall, with a shit-eating grin on her face, watching us! Chauncey's head was tilted back with his eyes closed, unaware of our audience.

I mouthed the words "Go away," and she stuck her tongue out and mouthed back "No," and covered her mouth, giggling.

I shook my head and refocused my attention on Chauncey. He pulled off his shirt and then lifted my dress up over my head, leaving only my Gucci shoes on me. Then he wrapped his arm around my waist and stood up while his dick was still deep in me.

"Where's your bedroom?" He grunted lustfully.

"That way." I pointed down the hall.

Kandi quickly darted back in her room before she could be spotted by Chauncey.

Chauncey carried me down the hallway while I was still riding his dick. He pushed the door open and walked in, and I made sure I grabbed the door and slammed it shut. Kandi's little nasty self wasn't going to watch the rest of our private show.

20

Judas kiss

College Park, GA

NIKKI

After my talk with Jasmine, I was happy she was onboard and ready to help us take down Malachi. Jayson was sitting a few tables away from us, pretending to read a book, and he had heard most of what was said. When Jasmine left, Jayson came over to my table, and I confirmed everything that we had talked about.

Now it was time for phase two of our plan. I had to give Polo the story we cooked up and make him believe it. Dre hated this part and didn't want me anywhere near him. I didn't want to be in the same room with that bitch-ass nigga, but this had to be done, and I was the only one that could do it. After finally convincing Dre that I would be safe around Polo, Jayson agreed to be nearby if anything went left.

I left from midtown and went back to my house in College Park. I called Polo and told him to come over. A few minutes later, Polo was ringing my doorbell.

I took a deep breath and walked to the door. "Hey, Polo."

"What's up, Nikki?" Polo replied and came inside and sat on my couch.

I closed the door and joined him on the couch.

"So you said on the phone you had something important to tell me about Malachi?"

"Yeah, you told me I should tell you if I overheard something important."

He nodded. "Yeah, what is it?"

I looked him in the eyes, and I could see the eagerness. *Snake-ass nigga*, I thought.

"Well, I was with Malachi last night."

Polo frowned. "You were with him?"

"Not like that. I was in his office when he got a phone call."

"Oh. Okay."

"I really couldn't hear what the other person on the other end was saying, but Malachi was stressing that he needs the shipment in on Saturday night. He said he was going to be there himself to make sure nothing went wrong."

"Shipment," Polo said aloud. "He found a new supplier?"

"That's what I thought."

"Did he say where this drop was going down at?"

"He said something about a warehouse in Hapeville, four o'clock in the morning. He said Airport Loop Road and Forrest Ave., the old storage warehouse. I wish I knew more details."

Polo smiled. "Don't worry about it, Nikki. You've given me all the information I need. I promise you I'm gonna kill that nigga for what he did to Dre."

The hairs on the back of my neck rose when I heard him say that.

For what he did to Dre? You dirty-ass mutherfucka! You shot Dre! You betrayed your best friend! You want to take me away from the father of my child, you bitch-ass nigga! I screamed in my head.

It took all my self-control not to take the razor blade out of my pocket and cut his throat, but I held on to my rage and I smiled.

"Thank you, Polo. I don't know what I would do if you weren't here for me."

He took my hand. "Like I told you, Nikki, I'm always going to be there for you, and I hope soon you let me take care of you for real."

I think I threw up a little in my mouth. "You don't know what it means to hear you say that to me, Polo."

Polo leaned in to kiss me, and I wanted to turn my head, but I let him kiss me. He made me sick, and I pulled away from him.

"I know it's too soon for you, but I can't help myself."

"I promise you, Polo, once you take care of Malachi, you'll get everything you ever wanted plus more," I said seductively, and Polo smiled.

I got up off the couch and walked to the door. Polo followed behind me, and then he did the unthinkable. This grimy nigga grabbed my ass. I wanted to slap the shit outta him.

"I hope this is part of the *plus more*," he whispered in my ear.

I turned around and faced him. "You'll find out very soon."

Polo grinned like an ugly little monkey. I opened the door, and Polo walked out. I closed the door and locked it.

The only thing you're going to get is the same thing you gave Dre: a bullet in your ass!

JASMINE

After the workout Chauncey had given me the night before, I was surprised I could walk straight. My pussy was sore, that much was for sure, but it felt so good.

I couldn't believe how fast I was falling for this man. Hell, any man. I loved women, and I thought if I had any kind of relationship in the future, it would be with one, but along came Nurse Good Dick, and I was begging for that old thing back like a fiend.

Chauncey had left an hour ago, and I dragged myself out of bed and into the shower. I pulled on my robe and walked out to the kitchen and saw Kandi cooking breakfast. She gave me a mischievous grin.

"I heard someone sing a new song last night. *Ooohhh, Chauncey, do it to me like that, baby! You blowing my back, baby. Your dick's at my G-spot. You making my bed rock,*" Kandi sang, remixing the lyrics from "Bed Rock."

"Shut up." I smiled. "I was not that loud. You must've had your ear to my door," I accused her. "I can't believe you were watching us fuck last night."

"How was I supposed to know you would be getting busy on the couch?" Kandi handed me a plate of scrambled eggs and bacon. "So you really like him, huh?"

I smiled and took a forkful of eggs. "Maybe."

"Bullshit! Nurse Chauncey got you open and you know it."

"Whatever. I enjoy his company. We click together."

She gave me a sly smile. "I know. I saw you two clicking hard last night."

"Shut up. I don't know. It's more than just a physical thing." I put my fork down. "He understands me. He doesn't judge me. I've never met a man like him before."

"I can feel the love in the air," Kandi crooned.

I couldn't even argue with her on that one. I was not going to force anything to happen between us. I was just going to wait and see what happened between us.

Thoughts of what Nikki had told me the day before still played in my head. This was the night to set things into motion. It was a risky move, but I really wanted to get rid of Malachi. He'd been doing too much dirt to everybody not to get his in return.

"Kandi, I want you to know you can stay here as long as you want, rent free. Just as long as you get back in school and make something of yourself. I don't want you ever setting foot in a strip club to work again."

Kandi looked at me. "I will, Jasmine. I can never thank you enough for everything you've done for me."

"Just you succeeding in life is thanks enough for me."

Kandi got up and hugged me.

Later that night, I went to work at The Pink Palace, and as I was walking the club floor, I spotted Hester and Jade. I hadn't seen those chicks since the night Kandi got in trouble. I blamed them, but the truth was, they didn't make Kandi get high. They didn't make her get in the car with Chaz. I just needed somebody to blame, and they were there.

I walked over to them, and Hester looked like she was ready to fight first and ask questions later.

"Chill. I ain't here to fight you," I said to her.

Hester looked me up and down. "What do you want then?"

"I just wanted to make it clear that there's no beef between us—unless that's what you want?" I paused and looked at both of them and they didn't respond.

"Good. I was upset about what happened to Kandi, but that was no excuse for me to blame y'all for her actions."

Hester's facial expression softened. "We heard what happened to her. We didn't mean for that to happen to her. I mean, we're not anybody's babysitter, but we wouldn't set her up like that."

"That's good to know, but you both know what shit can happen working here, especially to young girls fresh up in here. If we don't look out for each other, these niggas certainly won't."

Hester nodded. "I hear you. Is Kandi coming back?"

"No. She's going back to college. I'm make sure she stays on track this time."

She smiled. "Good for her. You're a good person, Jasmine. Too bad we all don't have you looking out for us," Hester said and walked away with Jade.

For some reason, it felt good hearing her say that to me. Shit, she was like the fourth person to call me a good person that week. I wondered if they all were seeing something I was not. All this time I'd been trying my best to be "that bitch," and I ended up growing a heart instead. How the hell did that happen?

The club closed at two thirty a.m. that night, so I decide to make my move up to Malachi's office. Bump of course stopped me at the steps.

"Wussup, Jasmine?"

"Wussup, Bump. Is Malachi up in his office?"

"Yep."

"I need to see him."

"About what?" he asked.

I smiled. "Business."

Bump smirked back. He knew exactly what I meant. Half the time I thought he had his ear to the door, listening to Malachi and me "conduct business" when I was up in there.

He picked up the phone on the wall and called Malachi in his office. After telling him I wanted to see him, Bump hung up.

"C'mon," he said, and I followed him.

Bump opened the door, and I saw Malachi in his chair, smoking a cigar as usual. Bump left and closed the door behind him.

"Jasmine, if you ain't here to fuck me, then I can't be bothered," Malachi said, still pissed I guess about the shit I had said to him last time.

"Well then, I guess I'll leave and keep this information I got about Don P to myself," I said and turned around.

"Wait. What information?"

I turned back around and had a seat in the chair in front of his desk. "I found out from a very reliable source who this Don P is and where he is."

"From who?" Malachi questioned.

"Nikki," I said and smiled.

Malachi frowned. "Nikki? What did she tell you?"

"Well, before we discuss that, we need to discuss how much this information is worth to you."

"Hmph. Depending if it's good, it could be very profitable for you."

"Profitable as in $100,000?"

Malachi scowls. "Don't try and run game on me. I'll give you $50,000. If it's true. Do we have a deal?"

I smiled. "That sounds good to me. Where's the cash?"

Malachi sighed as he leaned to his left and opened the safe in his desk. Then he pulled out a couple of stacks and threw them on the desk in front of me. I recognized the band colors that held the money.

"Got a bag?" I asked. He got up and got a small black luggage bag out of his closet and tossed it to me. I quickly put the money in the bag, but then I realized it's only half. "Malachi, this is only twenty-five Gs."

"Half now. The other half after I verify what you're saying to me is true. Now, what did Nikki say to you?"

It would have to be enough for now. "Well, you know me and Nikki have gotten very *close* these past couple of weeks," I implied purposely.

"You have? And why haven't you told me about that?"

"I never kiss and tell. Well, unless I'm getting paid to."

"Hmph. Continue."

"Well, first of all, Nikki really hates you." Malachi scowled at me. "She trying to find any way she can to get away from you, and she thinks she has. Couple of nights ago, after we got done . . . making each other feel good, she shared with me just how she plans to do that."

"What does this have to do with Don P?"

"I'm getting to that part. She tells me that she wants me to kick it with her and her new man, Don P. So, of course, I'm shocked by this, but I don't just get down with any nigga, especially niggas beefing with you. Nikki tells me he's going to take you out, and they'll be running shit after you're dead."

Malachi looked at me suspiciously. "So why would you tell me this? Why not go with them and kill me?"

"I'm not gonna lie. It sounded tempting, but then she told me that the man that's supposed to take you out and make this miracle come up is really that lame nigga Polo, going by the name Don P. I like the way things are now. I make lots of money being with you, and it's better to deal with a devil I know than one I don't."

"Polo!" Malachi yelled angrily. "That nigga that's been trying to get down with my crew is the same nigga trying to blood clot kill me!" Malachi slammed his fist on the desk, and it felt like he almost cracked the thing in two. "You sure about this?"

"Yes. Polo was Dre's best friend. He's always wanted Nikki for himself, and he hates you for killing Dre. Personally, I think you done him a favor, 'cause now he's fucking Nikki day and night."

Malachi got up and slammed his fist down on his filing cabinet. I'd never seen him this pissed before. I didn't know he wanted Nikki this bad.

"No wonder she decided to get brave and cuss me out. Her and Polo trying to kill me. Pussyholes." He turned and glared at me, and for the first time I'm afraid for myself. Maybe this wasn't as simple as I thought it would be. "Where are they?"

"I don't exactly know where they're held up at. Nikki been ghost the past couple of days, but she did tell me that Polo has a big deal going down tonight in Hapeville off of Airport Loop Road and Forrest Ave., the old storage warehouse, around four a.m. Something about finding an out of state connect."

"Pussyholes," he mumbled. "They want to blood clot play with me." Malachi picked up his phone. "Get Ricky and Reggie up here now," he ordered Bump and hung up.

I sat nervously in the chair, trying not to turn Malachi's wrath toward me. I could literally see the veins in his head protrude as he paced his office.

A few seconds later, Bump opened the door, with Ricky and Reggie behind him. Reggie had bandages on his head from the ass kicking Malachi gave him a few days ago.

"What's up, Malachi?" Ricky asked.

"I just found out who this pussyhole Don P is." He looked at Reggie. "Polo."

"What? Naw, that's not possible," Reggie said, scared to death. "I mean, how could he be?"

Malachi backhanded him across the face. "You dummy. He's been using you to get close to me. If you weren't such a fucking idiot, you would have realized it."

He held his face. "But, Mal, he was the one that shot Dre for you," Reggie explained.

"The nigga I told you to kill!" Malachi screamed. "He shot Dre because he wanted Nikki, and now that pussyhole wants to take my spot. Ricky, get the niggas ready for war now. We're going to Hapeville to pay Polo a visit."

"Right away," Ricky replied and walked out. Reggie turned to follow him.

"Where the fuck you think you're going?" Malachi yelled at him.

"I . . . I was going with Rick."

"You ain't going anywhere! I got other things for you to do!"

"Okay, okay," Reggie timidly replied.

"You're going to stay here and watch her." Malachi pointed to me.

I crinkled my eyebrows. "What? I got things to do."

Malachi turned and grabbed the sides of the chair I was in and got in my face. His breath was hot, and the look in his eyes was that of pure rage. "You don't got shit to do until I come back here with Polo's blood on my shoes. Then you'll get paid the rest of your money. And if you're lying, I'll put you in a hole right next to that bitch Nikki when I catch her ass."

He turned and walked up on Reggie. "Watch her. If she tries to leave, shoot her in the leg." He put his finger in his face. "Don't fuck this up."

"Yeah, Mal, I got you," Reggie mumbled.

Malachi looked at Bump. "Let's go."

Malachi marched out the door with Bump behind him and left Reggie to stand guard over me in his office.

Great. This was not how this was supposed to go. I could only pray now that Polo killed Malachi, because if he didn't, Malachi would kill Nikki, and maybe me too, for the hell of it.

21

I'm going in (and I'ma go hard)

Hapeville, GA

MALACHI

You try and murder me, but I will murder you.
Finding out that that little pussyhole Polo was the one behind trying to murder me wasn't surprising. I didn't trust any nigga. But to find out Nikki had been fucking him all this time was unacceptable and disrespectful.

This info coming from Jasmine was a bit suspicious, but Reggie confirming the fact that Polo was the one who shot Dre validated her claim—for now. I knew firsthand that Nikki's pussy was good enough to kill for.

Jasmine had no loyalty to no one except money. That was why I left Reggie behind to watch her. If she was telling the truth, then I'd pay her. If not, I had a bullet with her name on it.

In less than thirty minutes, Ricky had gotten together a group of niggas twenty deep, ready for war. I was going to oversee this shit myself so no mistakes would be made. I wanted to kill that pussyhole Polo myself, but before I did, I wanted to find out where Nikki was. I had special plans for her. She was going to feel my dick one last time before I murdered her.

I rode in a custom armored black Hummer, armed with my Mac 11 and .45 Magnum cocked and ready to murder. Bump was driving, and Ricky was in the car right behind us.

I'd done business in Hapeville in the past, and I knew the perfect spot was over by Airport Loop Road. There were a few secluded areas where you could do business.

As we pulled up in the area, I didn't see anything. We parked outside of the warehouse, and I motioned for Ricky to go check it out.

Ricky and Chaz got out of their car and ran up to the warehouse with guns in hand and checked it out. I sat in the passenger side of the Hummer next to Bump, watching them move around the building. Then Ricky and Chaz headed back, and Ricky shook his head, letting me know the spot was empty.

Shit! If that bitch Jasmine was lying to me, I'd make sure her ass didn't see the sun rise!

Just as I was about to signal for us to pull out, a barrage of gunshots rang out. Chaz was the first one to get cut down. His chest was torn open by hot slugs.

I turned and saw a group of niggas approaching us from the next building on foot. I ducked out of the Hummer and returned fire with my Mac 11, spraying them pussyholes up! I hit two, maybe three niggas as my crew scrambled around their cars, taking fire. We were taken off guard. A few of my niggas got hit.

Then I spotted that nigga Polo and I opened fire on his bumbaclot ass. "Kill these nigga!" I yelled as I busted my Mac 11.

"I got ya, boss." Bump went into the backseat of the Hummer and pulled out a rocket launcher, rested it on his shoulder, and locked his sights on Polo behind the crates. Bump fired the rocket, and a stream of smoke cut through the sky as niggas ran for their lives. An explosion erupted, and niggas and debris flew through the air.

"I got 'em, boss," Bump yelled as he took aim again, but before he could fire, a bullet tagged him in the shoulder and he fell to the ground.

These niggas flanked to the right of us, trying to surround us. I jumped back in the armored Hummer, protected from the gunfire. I looked out the back and saw Ricky get hit in the head. Shit, that nigga was dead! This was turning into a bloodbath for us. We were out-manned. They were waiting for us. This wasn't a drug deal; this was a fucking setup!

Now it was all about survival. My niggas were either dead or injured, and they were closing in on me. I knew that nigga Polo must have got hit by at least some shrapnel from that rocket blast. I had to get out of there. The keys to the Hummer were still in the ignition, and I ducked down and started the beast.

I glanced over and saw Bump still alive but in pain on the ground on his back. He grabbed the rocket launcher and aimed it at the niggas closing in, and he fired again. Another explosion erupted, and body parts hit the ground like we were in Iraq. He gave me the opening I needed, and I mashed down on the gas and ran over a nigga who was thrown to the ground after the blast.

I burst through the metal fence and onto the road. Gunshots bounced off of the Hummer as I took off down the street. I had made it, and the only thing on my mind was vengeance. That bitch Jasmine was going to pay with her life for this shit!

JASMINE

This was not how this shit was supposed to go down. It had been almost an hour since Malachi left me with

Reggie watching over me in his office. The club was
empty and closed for business. I knew I couldn't just
sit there and wait for whatever to happen. My phone
had been vibrating in my purse, but I couldn't dare
check it. Reggie was the key to my freedom. He was
just sitting in Malachi's chair, eyeing me up and down
while texting on his phone.

"So how long are you going to let Malachi bully you
like this?" I asked him.

"Shut up."

"Is that your response? C'mon, Reggie. How do you
ever expect to be your own man if you keep on letting
Malachi treat you like his little bitch?"

Reggie glared at me. "I ain't his bitch! He's my
brother and he looks out for me."

I chuckled. "Is that what you call it? That was fucked
up what he did to you in here the other day. Why did
he go off like that?" I asked, playing dumb. I knew
Malachi had whooped his ass because of what I told
him about Nikki and Reggie.

"None of your business! And if you think you can
talk your way out of here, then forget it," he yelled.

I sighed and leaned back. If he had half a brain, he
would have listened to me and we could have cut a deal
and gotten out there with some money. I knew Malachi
had a fortune in that safe under his desk.

I sat there for another five minutes, not saying a
word, but then it hit me that I'd been trying to get
at Reggie the wrong way. His weakness had always
been pussy, and he'd wanted my pussy for months. I
was wearing a white mini skirt, a pink low-cut midriff
T-shirt that just covered my titties, and a cropped and
fitted motorcycle jacket.

I stood up and took off my jacket. "Mind if I
get comfortable?"

"Go right ahead."

I tossed my jacket on the sofa behind me and sat back down in the chair. Reggie's eyes were glued to my body. I leaned back and opened my legs, placed my hand between my legs, and started touching myself. I bit my bottom lip, closed my eyes, and leaned my head back.

"What are you doing?" Reggie asked.

"I'm relaxing."

He stood up to get a better view. "That's how you relax?"

I looked at him. "I'm bored and horny. I just need to bust a nut and I'll be good."

Reggie walked around from the desk, watching me, and grabbed his dick. "Need any help catching that nut?"

I stared at him for a second as if I was contemplating it, and shrugged my shoulders. Reggie came toward me and slid his hands up my thighs, touching my pussy. "Damn, you wet."

I gave him a moan, letting him think I enjoyed his touch. Reggie bent down and kissed my legs. I pushed him back, stood up, and sat on top of Malachi's desk. I leaned back and opened my legs, and Reggie stood between my thighs. He reached up my skirt and pulled down my thong, exposing my fat pussy lips to him.

"Damn, I always love the way that pussy looks on stage, but it looks so much better up close."

"Why don't you give it a kiss?"

Reggie smiled and went down on me. He licked, sucked, and slurped my pussy. Damn, this little ugly muthafucka could eat some pussy real good. It was actually feeling real good, and I did cum in his mouth.

Reggie was really getting into it, but before he thought I was gonna let him stick his dick in me, I spied Malachi's marble ashtray on his desk. I grabbed it and cracked Reggie upside his head while he was eating me out. His head bounced off the desk, and he hit the floor, knocked the fuck out.

I jumped up and looked at that fool and shook my head. Always a sucker for pussy. I grabbed my thong and put it back on, then went into Reggie's waist and pulled out his gun. I walked back around Malachi's desk and spotted his safe. I wasn't no safecracker, but I knew how to fire a gun pretty good.

I took Reggie's Glock 23 and aimed it at the safe lock. I fired and I jerked back. The lock had a hole in it, but it was not open. I blasted it again, and it tore open. Bingo. I grabbed my black bag and started filling it with the stacks of money. There must have been at least $200,000 in rubber-band bundles. I had hit the jackpot.

As I was emptying the safe, I saw some documents. I took them out and sat down in Malachi's chair and looked them over. It was the quitclaim deed to The Pink Palace. My eyes lit up. I always wanted my own business, and here was a way to come up and own one overnight. Now, I may not have been a safecracker, but I was always good at forging signatures.

I took a blank sheet of paper and studied Malachi's signature and practiced it. It was close, but not perfect. I signed his name about five more times, until I had it perfected. Then I took the quitclaim deed and forged Malachi's name on it, then signed my name on it, effectively putting The Pink Palace in my name. This wasn't a fair exchange; this was robbery! Besides, Malachi was either going to be dead or in jail sooner than later. I might as well run shit.

I quickly folded the paperwork and put it in the bag with the money. I dropped the Glock 23 in the bag and zipped it up.

I started walking out of the office when the door flew open and a gun was pointing in my face.

ANDRE "DRE" WADE

Jayson and I had a bird's eye view of the mayhem that had just gone down in front of the warehouse. Both Malachi and Polo were gunning for each other, and just like we planned, they fell for it.

Jayson got on his radio and called it in. There were plenty of men either dead or injured all around the warehouse. But then I spotted a green-and-orange Pontiac speeding away from the scene, and I knew it was Polo.

"Jay, that's Polo! I'm going after him."

Jayson looked at me and knew what I was going to do to him. "Be careful."

I nodded and jumped in Jayson's car and took off after Polo. Within minutes, I caught up to him as he turned onto the highway. If I was him, I would have been getting the hell out of Atlanta, but Polo turned onto 285 East. I followed behind him. He was pushing it, doing at least 80 miles per hour, until he exited onto Old National Highway in College Park.

That son of a bitch was heading to my house to see Nikki! He must have known she set him up. But little did he know she wasn't home. She was at the safe house, waiting for me. This traitor had tried to kill me. He tried to steal my woman.

Soon he turned off of Old National into the Stone Ridge subdivision and was heading to my house. I took a back road so he wouldn't see me coming. I cut my lights and parked down the street. I made sure my .45 was locked and loaded, and I hopped out of the car and cut through my neighbor's yard, hopping the fence.

I saw Polo at my back door. He kicked it in. I made a mental note to myself to get a storm door for the back. I followed him in, and I heard him upstairs.

"Nikki! Nikki! Where are you, bitch?" I heard him bellow. "I'ma kill yo' ass!" He was going room to room, looking for her.

It was dark, and I waited in the kitchen with my gun in hand for him to come back downstairs.

Polo jogged back down the stairs, and he froze in his tracks when he saw me pointing my gun at his head. My face was still concealed by darkness.

"Whoa, hey . . . I live here," he lied.

"You wish you did, nigga," I said coldly.

Polo's jaw dropped open. "Dre . . . is that you?"

I took a step forward so he could see my face. "Who else would it be?"

"But you . . . you're supposed to be—"

"Dead? You need to work on your aim, nigga. If you shoot a nigga, you better make sure he's dead. I thought I taught you better than that. But you never were a fast learner, were you?"

A panicked expression washed over his face. "Dre, Malachi made me do it. He, he said if I didn't, he would send somebody to wipe out you and your whole family."

"Oh, so you did the humane thing instead and shot me in the fucking back in front of my girl and my kid," I spit angrily. "You wanted Nikki so bad that you tried to murder me for her?"

"Dre, c'mon, man. We can work something out here. Listen, we can kill Malachi and take over his shit. We can run this shit together," he implored.

I chuckled. "You such a bitch-ass nigga. I can't believe I ever called you my friend." I shook my head. "We set you up, nigga. Nikki and I have been playing you this whole time. Malachi was supposed to kill you tonight by the warehouse, but I guess you being the cockroach that you are, you slipped through the cracks. Doesn't matter. I'd rather kill your ass myself."

Polo dropped to his knees. "Please, Dre! Don't do this, man! I'm your nigga! We boys!"

For half a second, I felt pity for him, and in that second of hesitation on my part, Polo raised his gun and took a shot at me. It hit the wall next to my head. I busted back, hitting him dead in his chest, right through his heart.

Polo jerked back then looked at me in shock before his eyes rolled back in his head and he dropped the gun out of his hand. He then slumped over on the floor as a pool of blood formed underneath him.

I walked up to him and kicked his gun out of reach.

"I told you, you needed to work on your aim, nigga."

22

Battle of the Sexes

Atlanta, GA

NIKKI

I'd been calling Jasmine for over an hour and she wasn't picking up. After I kept on getting her voice mail, I called Gina the bartender. She told me that Jasmine had gone up to Malachi's office, and a few minutes later, Malachi and his niggas raised up outta The Pink Palace. Gina said Jasmine was still up in there with Reggie when she was getting ready to leave. That sent chills up my spine. The fact that Jasmine was still up in there, especially with that nasty little wannabe rapist Reggie, was frightening.

Gina told me she would leave the side door open for me when she locked up. I knew it was going to be dangerous, but I had to go there. Jasmine was in a dangerous situation because of me, and I wasn't going to leave her there.

I made sure I was packing the little 9 mm Dre had given me, and I was off to The Pink Palace. Twenty minutes later, I parked in the parking lot and went to the back entrance. Like Gina promised, it was unlocked for me.

I took my 9 mm out of my bag and crept inside the dark club. I looked up to Malachi's office and saw the lights on but the blinds closed. Chances were Reggie was armed and I would probably need to shoot his ass. I had no problem doing that.

I went up the stairs and put my hand on the doorknob and made sure I was ready to blast in my right hand. I took a deep breath and turned the knob and swung the door open, pointing my gun dead ahead. To my surprise, I saw Jasmine walking out with a black bag over her shoulder.

"Oh, shit!" Jasmine yelled.

"Oh God." I exhaled. "I thought you were in trouble." I lowered the gun and put it back in my bag.

"I was, but it was nothing I couldn't handle. Girl, you nearly gave me a heart attack," she said, relieved.

I spotted Reggie knocked the fuck out on the ground with a big knot on his head. "Damn, what the hell happened to him?"

Jasmine glanced back. "Him?" She chuckled. "Just another sucker for pussy."

I smiled. "I'm not going to ask. Let's get the hell outta here!"

We made our way downstairs. "I see you got paid."

"That and then some," Jasmine confirmed.

As we turned the corner, Jasmine got hammered and flew into the wall. She dropped to the floor like a ragdoll, unconscious. I turned around and saw Malachi with a gun in his hand and a menacing glare on his face. He looked like he had just come back from a battlefield! His suit was soiled and he was sweaty.

"Bitch," he growled, grabbing me by the neck and starting to choke the shit out of me. He picked me up by my neck and I couldn't breathe!

"I'm gonna to kill your bumbaclot ass!" He tossed me onto a tabletop, and my handbag with my gun dropped to the ground, out of my reach.

He was on top of me before I could even move. I was being choked so hard I couldn't move anyway. He slapped the shit out of me.

"You wanna bloodclot fuck with me? Well, I'ma fuck you!"

He grabbed my belt buckle and tried to take it off. I tried to fight him off, and he hit me again.

I was no match for him physically, but then I remembered my other weapon. I reached into my jacket pocket and pulled out my razor blade, slashing Malachi across the face. Blood sprayed across the club floor.

"Aarrrrrrgh," he yelled and grabbed the side of his face, giving me a moment to roll off the table and run.

"Bitch!" Malachi screamed.

I heard thunder explode behind me, and three shots barely missed me. I ducked into the back toward the locker rooms. As I was running, I saw a baseball bat in the corner that the security guys used when somebody got too rowdy in the club. I grabbed it.

I could hear Malachi turning over tables, coming after me. It was dark, and that gave me a chance to hide behind the rows of lockers.

"I'm going to kill you, bitch," he roared, and my heart was beating like a jackhammer in my chest. "Then I'm gonna find that little bastard child of yours and slit his throat!"

Now, that shit pisses me off. Fuck you, nigga! You threaten my child and I'll kill you.

But I wasn't going to give him what he wanted, to yell back at him and tell him where I was.

"I was going to give you the world, Nikki. I was going to make you wifey," he said out loud. "But you betray me! Try to kill me!" I heard his footsteps come closer. "Now you gonna bloodclot die!"

I readied myself because I knew I only had one chance. His footsteps were much closer. I could hear him breathing hard. As quietly as I could, I slipped around the locker. Then I saw the gun come first around the locker, and I took the bat and swung for the fences!

"Aarrgh!" Malachi yelled as the gun flew across the room.

I could tell by the cracking sound I must have broken some digits. I jumped from behind the locker and swung like A-Rod for Malachi's head. That mutherfucka ducked, and I bashed the lockers.

Malachi punched me in the jaw, sending me flying into the lockers behind me. I dropped the baseball bat. My jaw hurt like hell, but I had no time to acknowledge it because Malachi grabbed the bat on the ground, so I took off running.

I headed backstage. I could hear Malachi right behind me, closing in.

"Aarragh!" I yelled, feeling a blunt object whack into the back of my leg, sending me flying forward, sliding onto the main stage. Malachi had thrown the bat at me. I hit the stage floor hard, and I felt pain all over. I looked back and saw Malachi picking up the bat and then walking toward me. I started to crawl away as Malachi walked up on me.

"I'm gonna bash your pretty little head in," he yelled and raised the bat over his head. He swung down, but before he could hit me, thunder once again exploded in the club, sending Malachi flying backward, crashing on the stage floor.

I turned and saw Jasmine holding a gun in her hands.

"I always wanted to shoot him," Jasmine said. She ran toward me and jumped up on the stage. "Are you okay?"

I exhaled and smiled. "I am, thanks to you."

"I owed you one."

She helped me up, and I put my arm around her shoulder.

"Is he dead?" she asked.

I looked at him and saw his chest moving. "No. You hit him in his gut."

"I was aiming for his head."

"We'll work on your aim later. Are you okay?"

Jasmine touched her head. "I got a hell of a headache, but I'm fine."

Jasmine helped me off stage, and we sat down in chairs. We heard the sound of sirens resonating in the background. A few minutes later, Atlanta PD came in through the back door. I'd never have been happier to see them.

Epilogue

Meet me at the alter in your white dress

Atlanta, GA

MALACHI

I felt pain like I'd never felt before. My mouth was dry, my body sore, and I didn't know where I was. I looked around and realized I was in a hospital bed, and then I felt handcuffs around my wrists. I was hand-cuffed to the bed railing. I spotted two police guards standing at my door, and a nurse checking my vitals.

I tried to speak. "Wa . . . water."

The nurse jumped, noticing that I was awake. "Yes," she said and poured some water into a cup and then put it to my lips. I sipped as much as I could. "We didn't expect you to wake up so early after surgery."

"Surgery," I repeated. "Where am I?"

"You're at Grady Memorial Hospital. You just had surgery to remove the bullet from your abdomen five hours ago."

I remembered. I was about to kill that bitch Nikki when that other bitch Jasmine shot me. Then I saw a bag next to me. "What's dat?"

"That's a colostomy bag, Mr. Turner. The bullet destroyed your colon," she explained. "You should get some rest."

"Rest? I'm shitting into a bag for the rest of my life and I should get some rest!"

She stepped away from the bed, and the guards stepped closer. I was in no condition to fight, so I lay back.

"I wanna call my lawyer."

Two hours later, my lawyer, Jerry Powell, came to my hospital room. He was a white man who I used to beat any charges brought up against me. He was the best at what he did. For the amount I paid him per hour, he had better be.

He ordered the guards out of the room for a private talk.

"So what am I looking at?" I asked him.

"It's not good, Malachi. They have a lot of physical evidence against you, not to mention Ms. Bell and Ms. Dawson willing to testify you attacked them in her club."

I scrunched my eyebrows. "Her club? What the bloodclot are you talking about? That's my club!"

Jerry jumped back. "But . . . you signed the deed, Malachi. You signed the quitclaim deed, giving The Pink Palace to Ms. Jacqueline Dawson."

"That bitch! She must have forged my signature! I never gave her my club." I tried to sit up as I yelled at Jerry. "I want you to sue that bitch and get my damn club back, ya hear?"

"Malachi, calm down. If she did do that, that's the least of your concerns right now," Jerry explained.

"What do you mean?"

"The DA's office has a star witness willing to turn state's evidence against you. They're looking to prosecute you on RICO law. It provides them the ability to prosecute you under extended criminal penalties and civil cause of action for acts performed as leader of an ongoing criminal organization," Jerry explained.

"Who is their witness?"

Jerry swallowed hard. "Mr. Reginald Turner. Your brother."

JASMINE

I guess Reggie finally got tired of being Malachi's bitch and turned state's evidence against that nigga. I guess the witness protection program was better than twenty-five to thirty years in prison.

I completely worked with the police and gave them my story of buying the club from Malachi and him attacking Nikki and myself, and they ate it up. Besides, with the charges he was facing, he didn't have time to worry about *my* club.

The best part of this whole situation was that with the money I got from Malachi, I was able to completely pay off Kandi's college tuition at Clark. Now she could just go to school and not worry about anything other than getting her degree.

The money I was now making from The Pink Palace was more than enough to make up the difference. After being closed for three weeks, I reopened the club under new management. Not only was the reopening a big hit, but also I was now getting the respect from everybody as a businesswoman. I even made Hester the den mother of the club, and it was her job to look after the girls and make sure they weren't taken advantage of by anyone.

My days of dancing on the stage were over. The only one I was dancing for was Chauncey. Yes, we were still dating, and dare I say it? I loved him.

I started talking to my father again after the encouragement of Chauncey, Kandi, and my mother. We were now taking baby steps in reconnecting as father and daughter. After my parents found out I was the club owner and not a dancer anymore, they felt a lot better.

I'd learned a lot being friends with Nikki over the last few months. I felt like she was a sister I could confide in whenever I needed somebody to talk to. We were very like-minded in a lot of ways.

Today I closed The Pink Palace to the public, and I was having a private party for my new friends, Nikki and Dre. Well, not just a party. It was their wedding reception!

NIKKI

I couldn't believe how nervous I was. It felt like this day was never going to come, but after we cleared things up with the whole Polo and Malachi mess, the first thing Dre wanted to do was marry me.

After Dre killed Polo's snake ass, he called Jayson, and he was the first officer on the scene. Because Polo broke into our home and fired his gun at Dre, the police said his killing was self-defense, and no charges were brought up against him.

Malachi was convicted under RICO law for running a criminal organization and murder. He was sentenced to twenty-five to life in federal prison. His brother Reggie was the prosecution's star witness, and this nigga told everything. He was probably now living in Montana on a farm in the witness protection program.

Today was my day, my wedding day, and everybody was at our church in College Park in attendance. Janelle was my maid of honor and Penny, Jasmine, and Kandi were my bridesmaids. Jayson was Dre's best man, and even little Tyler was one of his daddy's groomsmen.

The time was finally here, and I took the long walk down the aisle in my white lace Vera Wang dress. Dre looked like a king in his Sean John tuxedo, waiting for me.

"I, Nicole Bell, take you, Andre Wade, to be my husband, to have and to hold from this day forward, for better or for worse, for richer, for poorer, in sickness and in health, to love and to cherish, from this day forward, until death do us part," I said with a tear tugging my eye.

The preacher looked at Dre. "You may now place the ring on her finger."

Dre slid the ring on my finger. "I, Andre Wade, take you, Nicole Bell, to be my wife, to have and to hold from this day forward, for better or for worse, for richer, for poorer, in sickness and in health, to love and to cherish, from this day forward, until death do us part."

"Well, I guess it's only one thing for me to say: Andre and Nicole, by the powers vested in me by God and the State of Georgia, I now pronounce you man and wife. You may kiss your beautiful bride!"

Dre lifted my veil and gave me the sweetest kiss I'd ever felt. I couldn't believe that I was now Mrs. Nicole Wade. This was the happiest day of my life.

ORDER FORM
URBAN BOOKS, LLC
97 N18th Street
Wyandanch, NY 11798

Name (please print):_____

Address: _____

City/State: _____

Zip: _____

QTY	TITLES	PRICE

Shipping and handling: add $3.50 for 1st book, then $1.75 for each additional book.

Please send a check payable to:

Urban Books, LLC

Please allow 4-6 weeks for delivery